Desirable Body

Hubert Haddad

Translated from the French by Alyson Waters

Yale UNIVERSITY PRESS · NEW HAVEN AND LONDON

A MARGELLOS
WORLD REPUBLIC OF LETTERS BOOK

The Margellos World Republic of Letters is dedicated to making literary works from around the globe available in English through translation. It brings to the English-speaking world the work of leading poets, novelists, essayists, philosophers, and playwrights from Europe, Latin America, Africa, Asia, and the Middle East to stimulate international discourse and creative exchange.

Yale University Press books may be purchased in quantity for educational, business, or promotional use. For information, please e-mail sales.press@yale.edu (U.S. office) or sales@yaleup.co.uk (U.K. office).

Set in Baskerville MT and Nobel types by Tseng Information Systems, Inc., Durham, North Carolina.
Printed in the United States of America.

Library of Congress Control Number: 2017963807
ISBN 978-0-300-22436-8 (paper : alk. paper)

A catalogue record for this book is available from the British Library.
This paper meets the requirements of ANSI/NISO Z39.48-1992 (Permanence of Paper).

10 9 8 7 6 5 4 3 2 1

Desirable Body

Reflection belongs to the head alone,
but the entire body has memory.
—Joseph Joubert

Prologue

Soon immortality will no longer hold any secrets for humankind. It has already been found in nature, in an insignificant jellyfish, the turritopsis; this jellyfish has neither heart nor brain, and once it has reached sexual maturity its life cycle reverses and it returns to a juvenile state, before it matures yet again, and this goes on forever. Everything that science has promised us will inevitably come to pass. In probable conjunction with bionics, transplant surgery will be able to reconstitute an entire person, just as in a certain gothic novel. A chosen few—whether fortunate or martyred—will thus be able to experience several consecutive lives with one and the same head, pathfinders for a perennial humanity. However, in order to answer questions about the use of a lover's body and the wholeness of consciousness or the soul, one must undergo the experience oneself, in the flesh, like a guinea pig for all eternity.

Perhaps some day far in the future, if biodiversity allows for it, when the human species has emerged from its coma and completely rewound the clock of the apocalypse, children and idiots will ask with complete candor what the world was like before the creation of human beings.

1.

He doesn't really recognize this city despite its almost worrisome air of familiarity; no doubt it has something to do with the time of day, the chiaroscuro outlining the facades in the evening light. Nonetheless, it is with steady steps that he reaches the Solitude Hotel, where as far as he can recall a room has been reserved for him. In the deep blue of dusk, the neon signs stand out above the rooftops against a background of mountains.

There are still crowds, young couples and old men in mourning, disabled people of all sorts, cohorts of nuns in cornettes as excited as schoolgirls. While he is walking on a high stone bridge across a roaring river that crashes against the pillars of the arches, a black-clad individual touches his shoulder in the semi-darkness. Startled, he leaps backward. "What is it? What do you want from me?" he exclaims, wary. He thinks he noticed the man a short while ago in front of the station, both of them standing about waiting in vain for a taxi. The other man probably followed him all the way to this poorly lit bridge. "Are you Cédric Allyn-Weberson?" the man asks calmly. He then notices the man's careful dress and the compassionate veneer of a mortician on his bluish face. "Let me introduce myself," the man continues. "Mr. Puith, Esquire, trial lawyer. But it is not as a lawyer that I have come to . . ." Puith grabs his arm, muttering empty apologies as he drags him to the well-lit side of the city. Along the way the lawyer, incoherent and full of allusions that are cheerful and quarrelsome by turn, speaks of a transaction or deal for which he claims to be the agent. All of a sudden, with a glass in hand, he becomes very friendly in the hotel bar and explains his mission more clearly: someone wants to buy from Cédric Allyn-Weberson the rights to the exclusive use of his name. Nothing less than that. A Texas financier was offering a considerable sum for Cédric Allyn-Weberson to give his name to him. "You see," continued the bizarrely slurred voice of the lawyer, "this name has no equivalent; you are the only one who's had it since your father's sudden death . . ." Long, wordy dreams are rare; normally we wake up rather quickly when distinct words reach our consciousness. His father's sudden death! He'd hardly had time to take offense before the scene faded into an uneasy listlessness.

It was with a sense of bewilderment that Cédric found himself in his bed on rue du Regard. The earsplitting noise of a passing ambulance pulled the last of him out of that halftone nightmare without his having lost its almost intact sequencing. He hadn't stopped laughing nervously since he'd woken up. The idea! Buying the name Allyn-Weberson because it is so rare—what gleeful presumptuousness! The ordinary absurdity of dreams had reached such a level of hilarity that it took his breath away. Was the dream linked to a secret wish to see his father die and thus free himself from the mark of an identity that was in and of itself despotic? They say all dreams conceal desires. Shortly afterward, in a sudden return to credulity but with a touch of apprehension, he turned on the television news. Obviously there was no mention of his father, except in a very roundabout way in the financial segment.

Cédric hadn't had any contact—at least not any direct contact—with Morice Allyn-Weberson for years, and that choice had been deliberate. While the old man believed he'd finished with his excessive, even devastating generosity toward a son with no special talents, he still had the means to interfere at will in Cédric's life and to spy on him through every keyhole. This was before fate got hold of Cédric, before the event that might horrify even a person condemned to hell and overwhelmed by its torments. Cédric readily admitted that being born rich could help overcome the most unforeseeable obstacles—for example, surviving either being abandoned or no longer having a body. But his story clearly demonstrates that there is no miracle cure against fate, even those cures concocted by the M. A.W. laboratories, the biggest in their class in the pharmaceutical industry.

2.

When, by some phenomenal accident of gametes, you happen to be the only son of Morice Allyn-Weberson and his tragic wife, née Erguson, the world seems to be a blood-red carpet that unfurls continuously at your feet. Without conceit of any sort, the protagonist of this dark tragedy could claim to have had a privileged, if not a happy childhood, despite the fact that his distressing mother had tried to hang herself on the eve of his twelfth birthday before finally throwing herself out the window in front of her husband. For a long time, Cédric's last name had been a blessing, opening doors for him, until one day, unable to tolerate it any longer, he'd stormed out of the family home and adopted in desperation a pen-name that suited him, a sort of sobriquet of solitude that he took partly from his maternal side.

It was under the pseudonym Cédric Erg that he would make a name for himself as an irrepressible polemicist back in the recent past when his father, without Cédric's knowledge, was watching over him with the one hundred eyes of the divine Argos.

This story, which would simply have been a minor news item if it hadn't put the future of humanity at stake, incidentally poses a few literary ethical questions: What, in fact, is the point of recounting in detail these unfortunate vicissitudes of a life whose outcome can only mortify sensitive beings? Honestly, we would be very worried if the explanation didn't count among our normal deficiencies. No one is responsible for the destiny of another, and even less so for another's misfortunes. Yet if but one single reader can manage to conceive in the loamy depths of his brain what that unfortunate Cédric Erg had to suffer, he would find himself reconciled, on an unpredictable or at least virtual plane, to this inconceivable, or even nonexistent, side of our poor human condition. Little does it matter if this man existed in reality—let us place our bets on the existence of someone who aspires to the distractions of happiness; whatever the case, the spate of catastrophes he would have suffered would correspond to nothing that could be admitted or borne by the average person.

After majoring in law in college and some less than systematic studies in political economy and comparative literature—studies that only served to delay indefinitely his taking on responsibility of any sort—this apostate son had been writing a column for one of the most prominent news magazines for eight years. By some mysterious stroke of luck, the last of the Allyn-Webersons received his press card before he'd written a single line under his pen name. Cédric Erg was not lacking in axes to grind. Having authority over the chaos of signs and events through the use of platitudes was to his mind the ultimate delusion, but his colleagues appreciated his courage and his free spirit. While his bêtes noires were all the predatory industries, such as the Big Pharma companies or the oil corporations, the politically powerful feared him even more, for he was scathing when it came to those jesters, investors, and other fat cats.

Impressed with his new recruit, the magazine editor gave Cédric freedom to betray his caste to the full extent, provided he never, ever revealed his true identity. "You would lose all credibility, and also risk your neck," he said to him with some alacrity.

3.

The young woman barely greeted him in the elevator. Ill at ease, Swen Geislar stood tall on the tip of his left toe and craned his neck to give himself a somewhat normal appearance. A few minutes earlier he had been sitting at the counter of the Vermont, the café across from the news agency building, and saw her drifting by in the sunlight; he had rushed in her wake with the gait of an out-of-kilter android, his eyes glued to the unyielding swell of her hips.

Lorna Leer had mobilized all Swen's faculties—mental and sentimental—since the moment she'd distractedly introduced herself to him in the big newsroom to ask about the weather in Slovenia, where she was supposed to go to cover a bloody attack on the French Embassy. She could have asked any transcriptionist on the floor, the way one inquires about the time, but fate had chosen him. When suddenly he found himself face to face with the most beautiful woman in the world, lightning passed from her to him, reducing all his common sense to cinders. If a minuscule amount of hope suffices to give rise to love, a heavy dose of despair can also make one person fall madly for another. The woman thanked him with an unforgettable smile, a pure gem that his memory would store in its jewel box. Ever since that day, whenever she appeared out of the blue from her travels, he'd spend his time following her like a limping shadow in the hallways of the agency or down the adjacent streets, ready to light cigarettes or open doors for her.

Lorna exited the elevator on the third floor with one of those melting, barely sketched movements of shoulder and face to signify a faint acknowledgment without a glance. Her perfume filling the elevator car was equal to a communion of the flesh. When he reached the fifth floor, Swen went to his desk, deaf to the distracted words of greeting from his colleagues, who were drowning in a flood of satellite information. In front of his screen, Swen clicked on the latest news in an effort to return to consciousness.

> Researchers conducting tests in the harsh environment of Mono Lake in California have discovered the first known microorganism on earth able to thrive and reproduce using the toxic chemical arsenic. This microorganism substitutes arsenic for phosphorus in its cell components. Upending all our knowledge about living organisms, this bacterium, which incorporates arsenical elements in its own DNA and in its cells, has just confirmed the hypothesis that previously unknown biological laws can exist on the earth and in the universe.
>
> Discovered in flagrante, a 37-year-old man was given a suspended sentence of one month on Friday by the court of the city of Nancy for stealing from the principal cemeteries of the region dozens of cherubs and Virgin Marys that he then placed around his dog's funeral urn.
>
> This past Thursday the United Nations estimated that the amount of oil pollution in southern Nige-

ria would require the most comprehensive cleanup operation ever known. According to a study put out by UNEP, presented Thursday at Abuja: "The environmental restoration of Ogoniland could prove to be the world's most wide-ranging and long-term oil cleanup exercise ever undertaken if contaminated drinking water, land, creeks, and important ecosystems such as mangroves are to be brought back to full, productive health." This unprecedented project will take between 30 and 40 years.

Two years after the surprising announcement in an American scientific journal of the possibility of transplanting a human head onto a donor body, Sergio Canavero, the chief neurosurgeon in an Italian hospital and expert in neuromodulation, is preparing to carry out this historic operation in the coming weeks. Using chemical substances that allow the regeneration of the links among fascicles of myelinated axons, it will then be possible to attach the spinal cords of donor and recipient and subsequently reactivate the nerve flow. A large team of neurosurgeons, plastic surgeons, and other specialists has already been assembled for the great day.

Grinning childishly, Swen didn't hesitate to change the neurosurgeon's name to Cadavero; all he'd needed to do was change a single letter, which we call a "typo." He took fiendish pleasure in adding this name to certain news items without getting into trouble, either because of leniency or blatant incompetence on the part of his superiors. His impeccable spelling allowed him these little flights of fancy at a time when he was required to correct the subjunctives, past participle agreements, and spellings of double-consonant nouns of almost all the editorial staff, including the editor-in-chief. As soon as he had some latitude, with his training in internet research and his skills in controlling sources and uncovering as much reliable information as possible, Swen would go digging around in Lorna Leer's online private sphere; however, to his constant dismay, he could find nothing amusing, provocative, or poignant. He would have loved to see her naked in some other life, a cabaret dancer or swimming champion. After much

Googling, copying, and pasting, Swen noticed the presence of the same individual at her side in a variety of settings. By targeting this newcomer, Swen ended up discovering his identity. It was indeed the polemical columnist Cédric Erg: a strapping fellow in a suit, six feet tall, who was gazing lovingly at Lorna with his dandy's eye. Sick with jealousy, Swen immediately diverted his digital stalking from Lorna to Erg. A good detective with adequate tools can always manage to uncover some inadmissible secret on the web. Even an angel would leave a trace of feathers behind. Yet Cédric seemed to have put up a solid wall around the image he'd forged of himself as a fearless and flawless champion of justice. Swen went back as many years as he could, but all traces of Cédric Erg disappeared early on. There was nothing on alumni or other social media sites of people seeking former friends. That rare last name, the meaning of which must be related to "ergotism" and "ergot poisoning," left Swen in the dark. By a bizarre coincidence that he wanted to attribute to some formidable system buried in his brain, Swen found a declassified document from a former patients' association that had been financed by pharmaceutical companies. It was quite simply about the columnist and his probable family ties to Morice Allyn-Weberson. The biography of the latter in directories and yearbooks set Swen on the trail of a first wife, née Erguson, and of an only son named Cédric. All that was left for Swen to do was compare his clippings to be sure. He had his revenge in hand. Lorna Leer would soon find out to what kind of traitor or spy she had taken a fancy.

4.

Still, it seemed as though none of Cédric's colleagues or readers had ever established a link between him and the M.A.W. company. Cédric had burned all the bridges imaginable that tied him to his ancestry, except the totally forgotten one on his maternal side. Only a monomaniacal detective with Asperger syndrome could have connected Cédric Erg to the businessman's wan first wife, long erased from memory. Morice Allyn-Weberson had moved close to Geneva, where his company headquarters was located, had remarried two or three times, and would certainly have divorced Cédric's mother had she not tragically anticipated his intentions.

Thanks to a new pair of glasses and a bearded chin, Cédric the renegade had completely transformed his face. Years went by, and no one pestered him anymore with compliments in the hope of receiving a favor from a super-rich relation. He'd become poor, almost impecunious: he had just enough money to pay the rent on a thousand-square-foot apartment on rue du Regard and to buy the best single malt whiskies. Though she envied his independence, his girlfriend could find nothing to criticize about their lifestyle. A slightly reckless field reporter who did freelance work for a large Parisian news agency, Lorna Leer was not offended by Cédric's penchant for secrets. In her opinion, her lover suffered from a kind of selective amnesia—he forgot nothing of what *she* confided in him. The couple lived an entire year in periodic intimacy between professional absences. The young woman understood, without its having been spelled out, the generic tragedy of Cédric's childhood. With her thirst for freedom, Lorna was accommodating by nature and expected nothing from him other than tender friendship and passionate embraces.

There are subtle shadings in our preferences,

everything fluctuates, love comes and goes like dreams or clouds. And so Cédric came to love Lorna with true passion the moment he discovered a beauty mark on her neck, just below her left ear. How can this be explained? It was a summer evening in Florence. They had made love gently, without that circumstantial savagery that lovers offer each other freely at the start of a relationship. As he lifted her heavy, amber-colored hair, Cédric was overwhelmed by unfathomable confusion, as if the meaning of the universe had suddenly been revealed to him without any other details. He kissed Lorna's neck at this spot, with tears in his eyes and the intense feeling of already having experienced this moment as many times as eternity could have reserved coincidences in time or space for some ill-fated immortal person. The young woman didn't notice anything; they fell asleep curled up together, skin against skin. This body breathing deeply next to him had just taken on immense sentimental value because of a beauty mark. Did he love this marvelous Lorna for herself, in whom he'd just discovered, by chance, right below her left earlobe, a sort of secret identity? Soon he too fell asleep, his face in her hair, thinking that no one is really loved because we constantly go to the wrong house or the wrong person with the same extraordinary obstinacy.

5.

A sudden hailstorm swept across the half-open metal shutters with the sound of a booming waterfall. Cédric Erg immediately recalled his nightmare, the poorly lit bridge and the businessman who looked like a mortician. He'd lost everything with Lorna, not just his physical appearance. She was and remained the vibrant sensitivity of his soul, or of whatever took its place somewhere inside his skull. Lying fully clothed on his unmade bed, staring at the ceiling, Cédric took in the glimmers of light outside that were blurred by the din of the downpour. How could the adventure be summed up? Ever since he'd met Lorna, he'd found stability and no longer questioned his identity. His research for his weekly column required real determination, given the various kinds of pressure and blackmailing that his revelations almost always triggered. Cédric didn't merely content himself with reporting allegations based on vague rumors; he delivered undeniable proof. Everyone, for example, might have caught wind of the fact that entire populations were wiped out in order to exploit new uranium mines; Cédric provided quotes and names. His favorite target, the pharmaceutical companies, constantly sent unambiguous signals to this maverick of accusations. Threats of a lawsuit and other intimidations left him stone cold, or, rather, surrounded by a haze. He was certainly spied on; and unless it had been some crazy coincidence, he could swear that an attack had even been made on his person. For a while now he'd been taking certain precautions. But the fact that he'd obtained a gun permit and systematically used rental cars did little to change his usual habits. The risks of the job were simply part of the job. The minute an investigative journalist begins to deal with conspiracies involving industry, finance, and politics, he knows exactly what is in store for him. Cédric's professional life in fact had little substance compared to his passion for Lorna, who was sensual, now madly in love and so forcefully present that all day long his mind was filled with pictures of her nakedness, her face, that beauty mark beneath her earlobe.

His father, as accustomed to Cédric's escapades as he was hostile to his journalistic activities, left him more or less alone from then on, even if his informants, managers, and subordinates of all kinds were still quite probably on duty.

Everything happened during the first days of spring. Not the slightest forewarning; no star of fate ever announces ahead of time a private drama or tragedy. On the contrary, Cédric Erg was swimming in happiness. Aboard the *Evasion,* a five-sailed pleasure boat heading from Athens to the Cyclades for a weeklong journey in good company, he had thought he could at last relax and lay down his arms. It was evening, and they were on the bridge facing the reefs in front of the golden island of Paros.

"We'll get married whenever you'd like, Lorna," he said without thinking, in the exhilaration of a charmed moment. "You are definitely the love of my life . . ."

The young woman didn't respond right away. Her smile was sad as she squeezed his hand, her immense blue-gray eyes turned toward him. Minuscule in the high yardarms, sailors were furling sails or repairing some minor damage caused by an inauspicious collision as they were leaving the Athens port. One could hear a rowdy chant broken up by the breeze and the cries of several gulls.

"Actually, I believe we're going to break up," she responded at last, in a trembling voice.

Cédric understood from her gaze that she was telling the truth, and it hit him with a slightly unreal, softened blow that he was still far from internalizing but that would devastate him, as if he'd glimpsed from afar the crest of some malevolent wave. Without answering her, teetering slightly because of the swell, he went to stroll around the mizzenmast on the foredeck swept with sea spray and abandoned by the pleasure boaters. Above, sailors were still maneuvering on the mast. Suddenly there was an ominous crack, up near the crow's nest. A cigarette in his lips, Cédric heard a ripping noise accompanied by a strong hissing sound that stopped when it hit his back so violently that he felt only a sort of prodigious chill in the dull explosion of all his senses, thinking for a quarter of a second about what a beheaded person must feel when the ax falls. His cries, smothered by the sea swell, mixed with the squawking of the gulls; but the sailors, who had seen a support of wood and scrap iron fall from the crow's nest, shouted much more loudly.

Passengers and crew hurried to the foot of the mizzenmast. Hands reached out toward the victim, whose legs were bathing in sea foam. An officer ordered everyone not to touch the mass of steel that lay across the injured body. Luckily there was a doctor on board. Lorna, in a state of shock, had lost her hauteur and was sobbing breathlessly. A steward was asked to bring her to her cabin while Cédric was receiving first aid. An hour later, after he'd been brought to Paros on a lifeboat belonging to the maritime police, a helicopter transported Cédric Erg to a hospital in Athens.

6.

Anesthesiologists and surgeons took turns in the operating room, diligent but not hopeful: so much patching up seemed doomed to fail, yet the brain scan showed some cerebral activity. The patient, who was on life support, had several serious fractures and other injuries. After a host of expert opinions, two specialists of spinal cord injuries attended to what was most urgent: decompressing the spinal cord and stabilizing the vertebrae. However, the discovery of a double cervical tear had considerably slowed the choreography of useful gestures to the point where Dr. Andreas Agno, the ER surgeon, had to revive the flagging energy of the staff with some strong words. Three teams followed one after the other once the neurosurgeons had temporarily withdrawn; a fracture or a wounded organ could be just as fatal as an embolism. The patient, placed in a medically induced coma as low as possible on the Glasgow scale, would probably not pull through.

"That would be the best outcome," thought Andreas Agno as he removed his white coat in the sterile anteroom.

"He's fucked," said his colleague Emilio Panzi, without mincing his words. Panzi was a young Sicilian doctor on loan to the Athens University Hospital for his expertise in immunology.

The chief surgeon waved his hand in annoyance, but then immediately let his arm drop.

"I suppose so," Agno admitted. "If he were to survive, it would be terrible for him and his friends and family, but our role is to try to do everything possible to that end, is it not?"

Raising his forehead, Emilio Panzi looked into the gray eyes of the Greek man and realized he wasn't expecting an answer.

"Do you speak English?" Agno added. "Then go find Miss Leer in the waiting room and tell her whatever you think is appropriate. There are situations in which giving people a sense of hope or one of hopelessness boils down to the same thing . . ."

It must have been 2:00 a.m. when Cédric Erg was taken from the operating table and placed in a room in the ICU from which the body of a young motorcyclist who had died the previous day had just been removed. The young surgeon assigned the dreadful role of announcing the news to a woman who was probably about to become a widow returned from that task extremely agitated. Lorna, breathlessly beautiful despite the dozens of hours she'd spent in an uncomfortable and badly ventilated room, did not flinch when she heard his verdict. Panzi had learned to show he had no illusions in critical situations, unless of course some miracle were to occur. But this time, clinical death seemed imminent to him. "I don't think he will last the night," he declared calmly, after giving the usual summaries about the patient's state and the procedures that had been done. Lorna's deep-blue eyes shone strangely.

"He will live," she whispered, the points of her pupils piercing the man's heart.

"But his is a hopeless case," he allowed himself to say.

"He cannot possibly die now!" said the young woman in a tone that brooked no argument.

She asked to see her boyfriend immediately, even if only through a pane of glass. Panzi didn't know how to counter this commanding beauty's breach of regulations. Under her spell, he broke the rules almost unconsciously, and took her into a decontamination chamber where Lorna slipped on a smock and plastic gloves; then he led her to Room 27 in the Intensive Care unit. Cédric was in a deep coma, his eyelids squeezed tightly shut; he seemed to be meditating on the terrible nightmare of reality. Intubated and hooked up to all sorts of equipment, he was breathing by means of a kind of imposed violence, a lab rat in his own survival.

Lorna touched his hand with her fingertips.

"He looks like a torture victim," she said.

"We must be prepared for anything: a drop in

blood pressure or a lack of oxygen could aggravate his wounds . . ."

The surgeon studied the young woman. He could have explained what the future would be: total paralysis, suffocation, spasms, gradual damage to the internal organs, kidneys, bladder, lungs, sexual and sphincteric dysfunction. But his near-certainty of a fatal outcome made all words superfluous.

"Leave us alone. I need to speak to him," she said.

"He's in stage 3," the Italian man responded. "A very deep coma. Do you know what that means?"

"That's my business. Leave us alone . . ."

Dr. Panzi asked her to be brief, then thought that, really, it didn't matter, that she could even rip out all those tubes and wires like any of the Three Fates: nothing of *this* man's fate would be changed in any noticeable way.

When she was alone, but with the door kept ajar as required in the ICU, Lorna leaned very close to her lover's face with its look of a drowned man, so dramatically peaceful. "Can you hear me? Do you recognize my voice? I love you, Cédric, I've never stopped loving you, but we could no longer live together; there were too many habits between us, we could no longer fall asleep like that, blindly in our love . . ." She continued whispering like this profusely in his ear, gradually liberated by so many confessions. For the first time since the idea of breaking up with him had taken hold in her without her having realized it, Lorna was confiding in him. Her confession had a kind of brutal self-indulgence about it, as if she hoped to go back on her betrayal, reshape it into some kind of lovers' conspiracy, but Cédric's inert body ended up bringing her back to her solitude.

"You'll live!" she said softly, as she rose to leave the hospital.

Outside, in search of a taxi, Lorna continued the diatribe in her head. A few days before the accident, she'd learned Cédric's real identity from an anonymous and no doubt ill-intentioned email, the truth of which she had no choice but to acknowledge. That chilling revelation had so wormed its way into her that she decided to break up with him. Cédric had been cheating on her for years with himself, with a stranger. But this duality no longer existed. Paralyzed, without consciousness, the body she knew even better than her own was being abandoned to a former emptiness in which all identities merge. Lorna turned toward the front of the Metropolitan Hospital, looking for the neurological services floor. Her gaze slid across the windows of the rooms. In a voice broken by emotion or anger she exclaimed:

"As sure as you are the son of Morice Allyn-Weberson, I know you will live!"

7.

A bitter wind swept through the Athens sky, revealing the surrounding low mountains and, visible from Mount Lycabettus, the port of Piraeus and its fleet of ferries. Lorna, in a taxi taking her back to the Metropolitan Hospital, contemplated the ominous blocks of concrete buildings cut at right angles from one street to the next, coiffed here and there with ancient ruins. She forced herself to pick out, in the anonymous mass of crowds mixing on the squares and the sidewalks overrun by markets, tourist restaurants, and shops selling trinkets, the face of a middle-aged man, any man, as the car slowed or stopped at a red light; she concentrated on the idea that she could have loved him, known him as intimately as she had known Cédric for years. What could differentiate this unknown man from the arbitrariness of the love of her life, if not the absurd imprint of habits? Lorna closed her eyes on that urban chaos that was so similar to the confusion of thoughts and impressions cluttering her consciousness. Twenty-seven days had passed since the accident on the *Evasion* off the island of Paros. How much time does such a tragedy remain suspended in reality, ungraspable? Cédric was not dead, even though he was forever pinned inside his skeleton. Still, she had to mourn the loss of the man she thought she'd known, and even more, of the man whom she'd loved physically and in every way possible. After her decision to leave him had rapidly faded on the sailboat, she became amazed at the inconsistency of human choices, which had little relation to the true anchors of feelings and passions. The taxi entered the hospital grounds, gliding beside the glass and steel building facades. An ambulance was parked in front of the Emergency entrance. Faced with the ordinary, two male nurses were cheerfully unloading an aluminum-coated stretcher. They were probably chatting about innocuous things while, beneath their grip, a life as fragile as a candle flame trembled between combustion and extinction.

Lorna turned away. Ever since she'd discovered who Cédric's real father was, an unpleasant sense of reality had come over her, along with bitter bewilderment and its aftertaste of pain. The Allyn-Weberson fortune had come between her and the brutality of facts. Now that she'd told him about the accident, the pharmaceutical magnate was no doubt going to take Cédric's fractured fate into his golden hands. Thus she would be freed of unbearable obligations. "Over my dead body," she thought, immediately frightened by the meaning of her words.

Wandering down the hallways of the neurosurgical wing of the hospital, Lorna thought she caught a glimpse of the chief surgeon; she hurried toward him, hungry for information, but his figure slipped away before she could reach him, and he disappeared into an elevator. Panicked at the idea that he was trying to avoid her, she stopped to catch her breath, then shrugged, saying to herself that, anyway, surgeons often took pleasure in handing out bad news. She found the section she'd been looking for and went up the hallway with its doors half-open onto hospital beds where a bare foot or the draped pyramid of a knee brought to mind the terrible loneliness of abandonment. When she arrived in front of Room 27, her flesh trembled with the fierce tenuousness of the moment. Cédric was sleeping at the bottom of an abyss and his lips were moving. Quadriplegic, incapable of uttering a sound, Cédric had come out of his coma a few days earlier, and his eyes begged for deliverance. Lorna was unable to bear the sight of his bandaged hands and puffy face; she turned to walk from one end of the hallway to the other, dazed. He had just uttered some words in his sleep, how could it be doubted? She had read his lips: Help, they said.

8.

Cédric Erg survived the three successive operations that Dr. Andreas Agno had scheduled out of sheer professional consciousness: Agno's sole aim had been to reduce posttraumatic complications. Having undergone the ordeal of those operations without any real change in prognosis, Cédric gradually went from patient to privileged guinea pig. He was in a teaching hospital, and because his spinal cord injuries showed no improvement after all that, he could practically have been the object of a pedagogical lecture on dissection. That's what Emilio Panzi was thinking once again while viewing the images of Cédric's cervico-dorsal junction and spine from the front and side. But that particular guinea pig had emerged from his coma and so was of no use to the laboratories of the young disciples of Galen of Pergamon and

Hippocrates. Panzi didn't really understand the chief surgeon's anger. Wouldn't he be freed of what was, in the end, a frightening responsibility? Top administrators had intervened to organize Cédric's transfer to a hospital on the Italian mainland, claiming that the patient's state necessitated operations "that required techniques not available" in the establishment where he was. According to the principle of free choice, Cédric Erg, who had recovered almost all his mental faculties, had given his agreement simply by blinking. Despite being a good surgeon and a cautious diagnostician, Agno was not nearly as capable as the potential Nobel Prize–winning surgeons in Turin and Milan.

Emilio Panzi raised his head toward a ray of sunlight, thinking that all this was no longer his concern. His year as visiting doctor would be over in a few weeks; he would go back to Rome with much relief and a few regrets. The ray of sunlight was diffracted as it went through the hall window and then penetrated the bay window of the reception office. A mauve figure was just gliding by behind the glass. It took him some time to recognize it: attraction and annoyance were battling inside him. Coveting the girlfriend of a quadriplegic patient upset him less than having to demoralize her. But it was indeed Lorna Leer, as ravishing as ever and even more than ever, because she had fine, tiny expression lines on her forehead and lovely violescent circles under her eyes that perfectly complemented her dark blue pupils. Exhaustion and anxiety in beautiful women had the charm of surrender. Returning from Room 27, Lorna entered the office without knocking, after receiving a slight nod from behind the bay window.

"I was sent to you," she said. "Any news?"

In a gesture of surprise as well as vanity, Panzi removed his glasses.

"What? Haven't you been told?"

"What do you mean?" asked the young woman sharply.

"Your boyfriend is being transferred to the famous Spalline Hospital in Turin, on direct orders from the Ministry of Health."

Lorna was relieved. She'd been afraid that Cédric had returned to his comatose state. But as long as Cédric's brain was totally functional, it was not absurd to dare to hope.

"When will he be transported there?"

"In a matter of days. You must know in whose hands he's going to find himself. You're the only one who can still put a stop to this infernal machine. But I suppose you have given your consent. Am I wrong?"

"Cédric asked me to."

"You know that a blink of the eyes is not equivalent to a signature."

"He would prefer by far to die than to vegetate in the state he's in now. He often spoke about this to me, as if he'd had a premonition . . ."

"Think about it! The whole thing is delusional! It belongs to the realm of science fiction. There is only the slightest chance that the operation will succeed, if indeed it takes place at all. There are too many requirements that need to be met in record time. And then, in our line of work, the first experimental procedures are generally doomed to fail, doomed to fail."

"Dr. Georgio Cadavero and several international teams of specialists have been working on it relentlessly for two years. In any case, that's what Cédric's father explained to me on the phone."

"The billionaire Morice Allyn-Weberson, right? We were all very surprised."

"I've never met him. Cédric is lucky to be his heir. I would have given my life for him, even if it isn't worth much!"

"Yet you'd wanted to leave him . . ."

"Who told you that?" cried Lorna.

"When your boyfriend began to speak, his first words were about you. He said he loved you. He begged you to spare him, and not coldly to kill him. Those were his words . . ."

9.

The private jet that landed at Turin Caselle Airport was unexpectedly delayed on the tarmac because of a bomb scare. Dr. Mirami, the neurologist from the Spalline administration, showcd his annoyancc in thc ambulance the hospital had sent. Those bomb scares, which occurred now almost daily, would end up blocking society and ruining the economy.

"Just calculate how much time has been wasted in Italy alone," he grumbled to the skeptical nurses. "In airports, train stations, businesses! It adds up to millions, even billions of euros."

After a delay of more than two hours, the ambulance at last entered the hospital grounds in the evening. Dr. Servil, Morice Allyn-Weberson's right-hand man, who'd come from

Switzerland and been delegated to supervise the transfer, was becoming impatient as well in the neurosurgical services reception area. The slightest hitch could get him fired. It was with a sigh of relief that he greeted Dr. Mirami, who was climbing out of the ambulance in a rage just as the flames of sunset were spreading. The two men accompanied the stretcher to Room 7 in a special wing of the transplant department. The patient was given a powerful sedative as soon as he was settled. The Swiss doctor and Mirami, an enormous hulk of a man with a skull bumpier than the shell of an alligator snapping turtle, left the room quite satisfied.

"*Missione portata a termine,*" said Mirami.

"Well spoken!" sighed Dr. Servil, who now had to send his report to the disagreeable old man in Geneva.

The next morning, Cédric woke up very early, eyeing the rectangle of blue inside a high, narrow window. The sky was as deep as obliv-ion. Little by little he felt the crushing weight of his limbs, as if he were sinking indefinitely into soft soil. Nothing had as yet distracted him when two startlingly beautiful nurses came into the room. One of them was pushing a cart; the other immediately drew back the sheet on his nakedness.

"*Buongiorno, signore! La incomodiamo soltanto per la sua toilette della mattina.*"

They washed him and swaddled him in silence, seeming totally serene. Their hands, cold grass snakes, slid along his body while the women observed him as if he were some kind of transitional species, not really alive and not quite dead. He said to himself that his coma had spared him this ordeal for a long time. He could have felt less shame by pretending to be asleep, but he couldn't keep his bulging eyes off the dancing creatures who were handling him. The emptiness of his total infirmity—he was incapable of moving a finger or controlling his sphincter—made him hostage to a hateful hygienic regimen. He'd woken up in the organism of some kind of aching newborn with a too-heavy head that retained all the consciousness of his previous life. It was nonetheless impossible for him to move his arms or legs. Only his tongue moved, without his wanting or being able to speak. After having diapered him and reconnected his feeding tube, the nurses went out, leaving behind them the odor of ether and soft soap.

What would he become like that, trapped in his lifelessness? A thing that is dragged and pushed without one's knowledge? No one had found it necessary to explain to him the reasons he'd been transferred. He'd simply acquiesced to some bizarre stammering. In his condition, to consent was the equivalent of taking some initiative. The previous day he'd been shot full of powerful sedatives: a shot for Italy! His transfer had occurred while he was in a deep sleep. The color of the sky confirmed this more than the nurses' language or the Intensive Care cell. Now he was waiting, useless to the world, in unfathomable despair. Would he have to endure all this paraphernalia forever? He would have liked to die the way one falls asleep, by dint of concentrating; to stop his heart, the only living organism inside a hollow, soft statue.

The very muted song of a blackbird coming through the window suddenly attracted all his attention. From the visible branch of a beech tree, the melodious sequences followed one after the other, reedy, with the silences of a muezzin between them. The bird was improvising on an endless theme. This tiny, harmonious mechanism was declaring its desire to the living space around it. That radiant palpitation of sound waves arrived at Cédric from deep within a universal secret. Was it possible that musical emotion was absent from it? Cédric closed his eyes in order not to cry. He had lost Lorna; his arms could no longer hold her. A glass wall separated them. From now on caresses were forbidden to them. She would grow weary; nothing fades more quickly than physical intimacy. In fact, he didn't recall seeing her again here. Hadn't she said she would leave him even before the accident? Horror and fear wouldn't hold her to him much longer. What could a young woman hope for from an invalid? It was the end for him. He would have wanted to tear out the thread of his life with his teeth, clear out the space of his anatomical remains, and go down the liberating road toward death. Disappear! The word was pure sweetness, similar to the last drop of blood in a severed artery. But who would help him? He didn't want to live one more day, one more night. Who would save him from the abomination of being buried in the tomb of a body?

Several steps echoed in the hallway, and the sound of voices came from behind the half-open door. A small crowd of white coats entered the room shortly afterward and surrounded the quadriplegic. The tall figure of a doctor with graying temples appeared at the foot of the bed. Around him, attentive to the doctor's every word, a staff of surgeons and anesthesiologists with compassionate faces seemed to be posing for a class photo while a young woman with shiny skin and pursed lips typed on a laptop. Smiling broadly, Dr. Mirami agreed with all of Georgio Cadavero's recommendations.

"We will have the patient ready when the time comes, *dopodomani* or *entro un anno!*"

"I hope it will be closer to the day after tomorrow," the chief surgeon replied. "It's no small feat to coordinate and keep at the ready a team of one hundred specialists . . ."

"And it costs more than a day of filming at the Cinecittà," Dr. Servil added in French.

Cédric's eyes were mobile, and again he noticed how the doctors were using him as a clinical specimen, with a kind of paternal indulgence and little concern for his problematic condition as a human being. Even though he had some knowledge of Italian, his mind was confused by drugs and the lingering effects of the anesthesia, so he didn't understand much of what was being said. It was the flood of white coats that really intrigued him. There were hardly any students among them; rather, they were all seasoned professionals. The one named Cadavero addressed the group with a mixture of severity and caution.

"The operating procedure isn't very complicated," he said. "And we've thought through the ethical questions. Of course, there are strict rules to follow, but I'm convinced everything will evolve positively in the future. As for the technical feasibility, despite what our French colleagues think, we have amply demonstrated . . ."

An old doctor with a chicken neck gathered in a bowtie interrupted him in English, provoking a flicker of reticence in his mentor. Was it because the patient, all ears, was manifesting his surprise with a groan?

"We'll cross that bridge when we come to it, dear colleague," said Cadavero. "Mr. Cédric Allyn-Weberson obviously must renew his agreement. Everything we undertake will be perfectly legal."

10.

Lorna had given herself twenty-four hours to make up her mind. She would spend another night in this city whose roads could lead anywhere; on a whim, she could take the train to Turin or stay a little while with Emilio at his invitation. With its palace courtyards, its alleys dug out in blue shadows, and its ruins that turned golden at dusk, to Lorna Rome *had* been built in a day. From the piazza Navona to the Santa Prassede, from the baths of Caracalla to the Turtle Fountain, she'd strolled for hours carrying in her mind the image of a shattered body lying on a hospital bed; a man's body she had known so intimately. Floating above that nauseating shipwreck of flesh was her beloved's drowned face, ethereal in the dusty light. Intermittently, the sharp pain of his physical decline shot through her, so that she almost keeled over. At sunset, halfway between the Area Sacra and the Capitoline Hill, she practically fainted, her arms and chest supported by the alabaster base of a caryatid.

When she returned to her host's before nightfall, Lorna gave in to him without second thoughts, and, naked as on the previous day, she forgot her strolls through the city with a kind of blind vehemence. To be manhandled and penetrated without warning for once satisfied her completely. Unable to stop herself at the edge of her desire, she longed only to be worry-free and asleep, in the primal satisfaction of an embrace. The man withdrew with a movement of his hips and lay on his back, continuing to stroke his mistress between her thighs with his moist palm. With one leg and her free arm, Lorna fretfully sought out the coolness of the sheets. The cold sperm and sweat of a stranger repulsed her slightly, like a trace of death. She shivered with fatigue. There had always been for her a threshold of aversion to cross before abandoning herself to pleasure.

"Are you drifting away, Lorna?" Emilio asked.

"I'm too hot. Give me a cigarette . . ."

He picked up an ashtray, the lighter, and his pack of cigarettes. As he edged toward the night table, the muscles of his back, still shiny with sweat, bulged.

"Why don't you stay a few more days?" he asked, sitting up.

Lorna, her shoulders resting against a pile of pillows, exhaled a long ribbon of smoke.

"The operation is scheduled for Monday. I want to see him before then; it may be the last time."

Emilio Panzi cast a quick glance at the young woman's profile. She'd said these words with a slightly raspy voice, but with no apparent anxiety.

"You're a surgeon," she continued. "Do you think he'll make it?"

"Dr. Cadavero and his team seem entirely optimistic. But all outcomes are possible . . ."

"Be frank! What are his chances?"

"It's impossible to say. No one has ever attempted such a crazy feat."

"But what is his chance of surviving?" Lorna persisted, in a strangely neutral tone.

"In my opinion, almost none in the short or medium term. I have to be honest. I don't think for a moment that they'll succeed in reconstituting the connection of the spinal cord. Professor White's monkeys, which are the reference point, didn't even survive twenty-four hours."

"That was half a century ago!" Lorna cried.

Emilio put out his cigarette in the ashtray that lay between their two naked bodies.

"That's true. Science evolves. Today we're able to re-create organs using stem cells. With a solution of two polymers, it may even be possible to fuse nerve cells. But you have to face facts. Those marvelous chemical substances will no doubt make it possible to repair a certain number of neural pathways, but how can one connect in record time the thousands of fibers, each with its own role to play, between a recipient in induced hypothermia and a donor who is brain dead? Can you imagine what godlike synchronization those hundreds of surgeons and their assistants must have in order to hand off to one another in squadrons with the impossible mission of not committing the slightest error? Not even to mention the consequences of total body radiation and the problems of immunosuppression and psychological rejection . . ."

"They will pull it off! Cédric's father has paid them to succeed."

"Your Cédric is a luxury guinea pig; his head is worth twelve million euros, a mere trifle for a pharma tycoon! But rest assured, at least he will remain alive in the annals of medical transplants . . ."

Lorna nervously squashed her cigarette butt, her eyes turned to the dark slit of the window. One word too many would suffice for there to be no possible tomorrow. She would take the train for Turin at dawn. With the sheet pulled up under her chin, she told herself that you couldn't betray anyone with your body. People only grew apart, more foreign to each other than ever, with a slight taste of disaster in their mouths.

11.

After a psychological exam in the presence of a court officer, in the confines of his hospital room, the patient was asked whether he would agree to the operation as it had been duly explained by Dr. Cadavero. Convinced he would not survive, Cédric didn't imagine for a moment the possible implications and consequences: anything seemed better to him than this interminable torture in the petrified space-time of the body's prison. And if this adventure, by some miracle, ended up giving him back a tiny bit of his autonomy, at least he would then have the physical means to decide his own fate.

Once all those people had left his room, he felt an immense relief in the inaccessible zones of his mind. Everything would soon stop, and he would be finished with this wreck of a body suspended on the hook of a cervical vertebra. The great void of living about which D. H. Lawrence wrote would soon join the "vast void of the cosmos." In the well of infinite abandonment where he found himself for centuries of seconds, he became oddly lucid at the idea of the nothingness that was so near. Without changing the axis of his gaze, he pondered the dust dancing in a ray of sunlight that caressed his left hand as it rested on the sheet. So: the creation by beheading of a new species was going to take place tomorrow or the day after. They were going to slice off his head, and that thrilled him to the core. Cédric dozed off thinking about this, and quickly fell under the spell of a dream. Why was someone letting hot candle wax drip on his face? He had been severed in two on the black flat surface of some sort of grand piano lit by two candlesticks; the panic of not knowing in which part of his body his consciousness had taken refuge drew from him an inaudible and unlocatable cry: did it come from the gaping trachea above his shoulders or from his throat, which was attached to nothing? Far away, a woman's voice made the soundboard vibrate. When he opened his eyes again, he recognized Lorna's face leaning over him.

"Are you sleeping?" she asked, as a hot teardrop fell on his lips.

"Thanks for coming," he murmured in a voice hardly louder than his breath. "I think it's for tomorrow."

"The day after. I spoke with Dr. Cadavero's assistant."

"They talked to me about physical therapy, decompensation, psychological support . . ."

"Of course. Everything has been taken care of; you just need time and willpower after the operation."

Cédric would have liked to lift an arm to stroke his woman's hair, touch her living cheek. Did she actually think he would survive this crazy undertaking dreamed up in secret by a horde of surgeons in search of fame?

"I'm confident," said Lorna, as if she could

read his mind. "You'll get back your mobility, your joie de vivre, your work . . ."

Faced with the unbearable steadfastness of her gaze, he thought that the only thing that could make him hope to survive was out of reach from now on. How would he ever be reattached to his being without losing those thousand ties that gave a distinctive face to his love? This woman had accompanied him so intently and given herself to him passionately, without hesitating, in the most graphic way. A faint smile crossed his lips at the thought of the desire running through his destroyed body like an imitation of desire.

"It can't fail," Lorna insisted. "There are too many scientific stakes . . ."

"And financial ones," Cédric said, interrupting her. "You're the one who contacted my father after the accident, aren't you? How did you find out?"

"Who you really were? From an old passport left in an inside pocket of a briefcase. As a matter of fact, I was just looking for a briefcase when . . ."

"You did a search on the internet. You compared names and you found a Cédric Allyn-Weberson on a class photo . . ."

"Yes; well, not exactly. Some anonymous web surfer took care of doing that; I don't know why. But it doesn't matter. I was devastated when I learned that our life together was rigged. Such disloyalty! As if I'd been the cover or alibi for a spy."

Cédric looked at her somewhat perplexedly. In the state he was in, no identity could have prevailed, given what he was feeling. Creatures were born nameless, then died in silence. There was no one, with the exception of a few chance encounters and sometimes some embraces. Did birds or rats worry about their social identity? Still, he refrained from commenting.

"Is my father paying these people?" he asked with a sigh, distressed by the twisted insinuations that were firing up his brain.

"Yes! A fortune! And his associates are controlling just about everything. You've really nothing to fear . . ."

Lorna looked at her watch as she grew restless a few moments before her departure, which she had not yet dared to announce; she uncrossed her legs and her fingers lightly clutched her handbag.

"I love you," she said by way of farewell, without the slightest hesitation in her voice.

He watched her disappear and sensed deep within his shell of a body just how little the physiological manifestations of emotion disturb the rational mind. He recalled that Darwin had not attributed any more use to them than to the appendix and other vestigial organs. A superfluous inheritance from our ancestors. But through what magic did his brain, cut off from the rest of his vital energy, manage to register all the symptoms of love? He thought it would be better to have a lobotomy, so that all of love's suffering would be obliterated. His emotions were floating so miserably on his gray matter, like will-o'-the-wisps of memory. The day after tomorrow, he was certain, it would all be over for him; Lorna would vanish with the rest of the universe in one final spasm of adieus, thanks as much to the cursèd fortune of the Allyn-Webersons as to the dire irony of fate.

12.

The operation had been prepared with all the rigor of sending a sounding rocket into space. San Severo Hospital, which had just been renovated, was chosen both for its accommodations and for the perfection of its technique. Even though he was well aware of his reservations, Georgio Cadavero had accepted the proposal of Aimé Ritz, his old friend and distinguished colleague from the Medical University of Palermo. San Severo Hospital would reopen its doors to the public in a few weeks. On one hand, the clause regarding the location stipulated total discretion in the event of failure so as not to ruin the establishment's reputation. On the other, the hospital would benefit from the media splash that pulling off such a feat would undoubtedly create. Ritz had nothing to lose: ten teams of surgeons would secretly put his new equipment to the test in a kind of dress rehearsal. He had gone over with his lawyers all the legal implications that concerned him. Everything was in place; a helicopter had just transferred the donor body on its life-support machine. The owner of the property, a neurosurgeon in semi-retirement, had obtained the right—the least of favors—to be present at the crucial moments of the transplant. He was aware of his former student's ambition; Cadavero was, moreover, a peerless medical practitioner who had to his credit major advances in neuropathic sedation techniques. His notoriety until now had been based on his science or art of resurrection more than on organ transplants, a practice that certainly required highly skilled doctors but had become rather common. For example, Cadavero had managed to bring patients out of the "hopeless" diagnosis of a stage 3 coma on the Glasgow Coma Scale. Hungry for fame, he and his direct collaborators were engaged in the most spectacular endeavors. Ritz thought it possible that they'd rushed the schedule because of a variety of deadlines having to do with publicity, competitiveness, or simple exclusivity. The hysterical pressure of the silent partner, the enormous costs of leasing the premises, and the continuous mobilization of interdisciplinary teams all contributed to this commotion.

The procedure was in place just before dawn on April 1. All the operating rooms were ready. After everything had been meticulously prepared, the medical staff, consisting of three anesthesiologists, a few nurses, and an entire battalion of surgeons, moved about as if they were walking on train tracks with complex switching points. In Cédric's case, the general anesthesia would obviously not require assisted ventilation, at least not in the first phase of the operation, but rather a precisely calculated therapeutic hypothermia. In front of their control instruments, the medical team's attention was entirely concentrated on the proper irrigation of the patient's cervical area. Two operating tables were positioned parallel to one another under steady surgical lamps in the largest of the operating rooms, whose asepsis had been verified several times. The surgical machines, the anesthesia machine, the medical equipment trolleys where exceptionally precise electrosurgical knives were aligned next to other tools specially conceived for the procedure were soon in the hands of a throng of gloved men and women in sterile suits and masks. A fleeting wave of silence passed when the two bodies were set less than three feet apart. Then the most impressive ballet ever performed in an operating theater took place. Dr. Emilia Baldini, from the teaching hospital in Milan and one of the innovators of the use of polyethylene glycol and chitosan in the restoration of damaged nerve cells in the spinal cord; Dr. Mirami, whose claim to fame lay in his role in the neurosurgical division of Spalline Hospital; and even Aimé Ritz, the director of San Severo Hospital, had all insisted on participating in vivo in the experience, even if they would have to slink quietly away in the event of a setback. Around Georgio Cadavero, in the first circle of the mechanical surgery team that would hurriedly have to cede its place to teams of neurosurgeons, the tension went up another notch when the two bodies, one of a man in a state of brain death and the other of a man in a medically induced coma, were stripped bare to make the transfer easier. While those two bodies were of approximately the same corpulence, Cédric Allyn-Weberson's, atrophied by months of immobility, seemed very feeble next to the donor's body, which had darker skin and well-proportioned musculature. Beneath the donor's taped skull, the draw sheet that partially masked his face nevertheless revealed a well-defined lower jaw studded with the black hair of a nascent beard. The man's throat bore a dotted line marked in red ink. The flesh was cut to the bone. The first team diligently prepared all the muscle tissues, the blood vessels, the trachea, and the esophagus, while two other teams were positioned to sever the two spines at exactly the same time before the bodies were switched. While the donor was being detruncated with an electrosurgical knife, Dr. Cadavero and his team were identically operating on Cédric's body. In perfect synchrony, the stage of the double decapitation was timed to the second. A nurse removed the head of the anonymous donor as soon as it was detached. The blood and bodily fluids of his decapitated body were sponged away, and it was immediately taken over by the life-sustaining team and plugged into the life-support machines. When the severed head of the recipient, decked out with all kinds of sensors, clamps, and electrodes, was placed with comical speed onto the table of the unknown man, a new wave of terror went through the assembly. No doubt because of a suddenly very obvious logical quandary: this head by itself, which was being transferred under a plastic bubble, seemed more like the object or organ to be transplanted than that enormous body that had remained on the table in the sorrowful majesty of a torture victim. The head was what was to be transplanted! But a life depended on every second—the life of the recipient, everyone thought, as they cast doubtful glances at the inert body. After having placed the donor's slit throat below the recipient's sixth cervical vertebra and throat, which was cut below the thyroid and the larynx, it was now a matter of reconnecting the spinal cords of the saved head and the sound body according to the most daring procedure ever devised, while in an acrobatic shuttling back and forth other surgeons were trying to save the circulatory system, nerves, and ligaments before the essentially prosaic remainder of the repair work could take place.

Dr. Cadavero had told the journalists a number of times that the trickiest thing was reestablishing the continuity of the spinal cord. To the great displeasure of the ASPCA, the neurosurgeon Robert J. White had grafted the heads of primates onto other bodies of the same species a good half-century ago, but without being able to reactivate the neural pathways. Now, however, we had the chemical means to reestablish those infinitely complex links. With a wave of his hand, Cadavero indicated to the nurses that they should sponge the perspiration-covered foreheads of his collaborators. He scolded the person inserting the oxygenation cannula. For a moment, his mind became clouded and he imagined himself an orchestra conductor surrounded by cacophony, or a ship's captain facing the sinking of his vessel. Hours were spent around that operating table. Several minutes had been lost at crucial moments during shift changes; hands hesitated, some teams seemed at the end of their rope. Although the operation had been painstakingly prepared, it was still a question of double or nothing. The stakes were such that, for Cadavero, failure would be worse than execution by the Sicilian mafia. The sweat of panic was stinging his neck and eyelids. Too many investments of all kinds were putting his career, his reputation, his very future at risk!

Those few seconds of wavering provoked a massive adrenaline rush in him. With an irritable order shouted with icy humor, he regained control of the situation. The dozens of doctors at work immediately rallied like so many music boxes rewound by the same hand. The nerve tissues of the head and body were wedged together in proper physiological position and were now connected in every single fibril; the circulatory system had been reestablished after the connection of the arteries and all the jugular veins. The bone stock was repaired once the myocytes had been sutured. The hypothermia that had maintained the upper part in an almost lethal state was progressively reversed through the joint effort of the IVs and an oxygen intake. But all that was now merely a matter for the resuscitation mechanics! After so many experiments with beheaded animals and humans, the transplant of a living body on a consenting head had just been accomplished: a world premiere in this private hospital in Turin. Georgio Cadavero had a burst of exaltation, a flash of delirium almost, but his mood darkened rapidly as he imagined that the outcome could lead either to great fame or great disapprobation. He admitted to himself, when he left the operating room, that the short- and medium-term risks of rejection, despite all the innovative treatments, were greater than anything in the entire history of transplants. Not only could the body refuse the chemically unfamiliar head despite all the immunosuppressant medications, but the nervous and lymphatic systems located in the skull could also reject all the information coming from a network of unregistered connections. Without even taking into account all the other homeostatic parameters. But enough! *Basta!* Day was breaking, and the patient had just been moved to a highly equipped Intensive Care recovery room.

The neurosurgeons, their colleagues in vascular and plastic surgery, and all the additional personnel assembled leisurely in the conference room for a debriefing. Exhausted from this medical marathon, the ones who were most involved in it complimented each other with some restraint: the battle was not yet won even if the procedure had been carried out without a glitch, although the mastermind had been understandably tense. Cadavero went up to the podium, freshly shaved and wearing a suit and tie. His expansive forehead shone beneath the lamps; he was smiling ostentatiously and stooping slightly.

"Thank you, one and all. You were truly marvelous!"

Applause broke out, which he calmed with a broad, pope-like wave of his hand.

"It's not yet time for congratulations. The patient is alive; we'll bring him out of his induced coma in a few days if all goes well. But we're walking on an unknown planet; each moment brings a new danger. In the short term, a severe rejection of the transplant is to be feared. Nothing can be excluded: the collapse of immune defenses, the absence of reflexes in the brainstem, irreparable brain damage due to poor irrigation during the operation itself, all sorts of viral infections . . ."

Dr. Mirami brought up the possibility of a malfunction of the somatic and autonomic nervous systems, which would risk compromising the patient's rehabilitation.

"The human brain is like modeling clay! You've heard of neural prostheses; if necessary, they will allow us to solve any problem of nerve impulses and discordant faculties."

Aimé Ritz, rather optimistically, wondered how the so-called second brain would react; this was the name customarily used to describe the enteric nervous system.

"Let's wait until our patient's mind wakes up before we start worrying about what his intestines think!" Cadavero said, amid laughter.

Annoyed by the flippant comment, a young Neapolitan doctor renowned for his research on neural implant systems abandoned his usual reserve: "An eminent French specialist of facial transplants says that we are undermining the ethical pact in the absence of any previous experiments, because it isn't monkeys or corpses that . . ."

"Will ever make the progress of surgical science possible," declared Cadavero, emphatically. "Compared to what we have accomplished here, a face transplant is mere cosmetics! And let's leave the ethical matters to the thinkers and poets. Our role consists of saving lives in every imaginable way. We are modern Prometheuses!"

"But we must talk about ethics," the Neapolitan said, this time with less assurance. "Listen. I read somewhere: 'A human being in perfection ought always to preserve a calm and peaceful mind and never to allow passion or a transitory desire to disturb his tranquillity. I do not think that the pursuit of knowledge is an exception to this rule.'"

"What are you driving at with your little quotation?" Cadavero asked, as he poured himself a glass of wine.

"We know nothing at all about the identity of the donor or the reasons for his brain death. Did he have a family, children, a wife? Will the recipient himself be told these things? From a genetic point of view, if he survives, Mr. Allyn-Weberson will have radically changed his identity; he will be carrying the genes of a stranger . . ."

Dr. Cadavero sighed wearily, one hand on his ear.

"I can understand your anxiety, young man. But let me repeat that all precautions and safety measures have been taken; we did not begin such a process without a scrupulous background check, both from a legal and ethical point of view. Mr. Puith, our legal expert, can provide you with a ton of certifications. Now, we are all going to rest . . ."

Before reaching the cloakroom, wanting to prove that no allusion escaped him and that he retained his sense of humor under all circumstances, he added in a syrupy tone: "Don't worry. No one would dare compare us to Dr. Frankenstein. Science, human rights, and jurisprudence have totally evolved since the time of dear Mary Shelley."

13.

The first autumn snowfall stuck to the steep cliffs, casting a milky light over a river of mist beneath the infinite shrouds of the peaks. In the interior valleys, it was almost still summer; a dawn sun revealed dazzling views on the horizon, whereas at ten thousand feet above sea level, somewhere between fall and winter, the icy breath of the summits fell on the mountain pastures and forests perched at a tilt. Between the snow-covered Mount Dou and the Isangrin Pass, which opened onto the distant foothills of the Jura, in a small valley accessible by a winding road, the Rult-Milleur château raised its octagonal tower and gables above a landscape of cow hillocks and hummocks that seemed circumscribed, to a troubled gaze, by illuminated cumulonimbus clouds or an Alpine chain. Leaning her forehead against a window, Lorna stared in turn at those limitless spaces and the château grounds' dark cedar trees growing around a fountain shaped like a crescent moon. A sudden loud noise made the windows vibrate. Behind the tall branches, a helicopter rose in a slow spiral before flying off.

Startled out of her daydream, the young woman remembered that a taxi was to drive her to the nearest train station. She was expected in Geneva that afternoon. Over the past few months her life had taken on such an unreal quality that not even a novelist would have dared exploit it. These past days spent in the hotel wing of this luxury hospital that had become a hotbed of media buzz were the last straw after all the mental stress and extravaganzas she'd had to deal with since the accident on the *Evasion.* How many times during the weeks and months of intensive postoperative care had Aimé Ritz, director of San Severo Hospital, in ceaseless conflict with Cadavero's staff, informed her of alarming complications, or even of Cédric's imminent death! Just three days after the operation, believing no doubt that he'd already accomplished a memorable feat, Cadavero—that advocate of total body transplant—held a press conference at a famous national television station where he'd just recorded a speech worthy of a winner of the Nobel Prize in Medicine. Afterward the carabinieri had to be called in to protect the Turin hospital from a massive onslaught of Italian journalists and other correspondents come from the world over to get whatever interviews, photographs, or testimonies they could. From one day to the next, Cédric Allyn-Weberson became a public phenomenon; photos taken on the sly by an indiscreet garçon de chambre soon revealed the patient's double identity. The magazine where Cédric Erg worked put him on its front cover, and after that portraits of the prodigal son of the pharmaceutical magnate flooded in. Because the press and television journalists had no other information about the family, they hounded Lorna, who had been recognized as his mistress, thanks to the cutting and pasting of images posted online by some monomaniacal hacker.

For weeks, in an attempt to escape the inquisition that threatened to overwhelm her, Lorna had sought refuge in Rome, where, against all expectations, she took up again with Emilio Panzi. Panzi, obviously aware of the news of the Turin surgeons' remarkable exploit, had spotted her, despite her shawl and dark glasses, sitting at a sidewalk café in the campo de' Fiori at dusk on a hot September Monday. The lugubrious monument to Giordano Bruno cast its shadow all the way to the young woman's feet. Lorna let herself be chatted up, happy deep down for the distraction. The surgeon had the spontaneity of a recent lover, and his cheerful mood was a welcome change from the climate of anxiety and antagonism she'd suffered through on a daily basis. He brought her back to his place on the via dei Coronari, and for the rest of the week she hardly went out. Inexplicably, for a time physical love pushed her nightmares into the far regions of her subconscious. It was as if confronting the sledgehammer of sex in all its most animal dimensions distanced her from the images of decapitation and wrenching apart that had been haunting her night and day.

What had become of her lover's tenderly affectionate body? Had it been reduced to dust like some poor broken thing, along with the rest of the human debris from the surgical wards? Along with the other man's head? And this new body that she didn't know, which she hadn't yet been able to see, how would she manage to accept its monstrous nudity against her skin, accept that it would take her and penetrate her? Just the thought of it chilled her to the bone and drove her toward Emilio with the desperation of a drowning woman grasping at straws. She grabbed him, his arms, his flat breasts, the fullness of his sex, with the brand-new feeling of an unbroken wholeness, an ardent plenitude. How absurd was the Platonic myth of the androgen sliced in two like a hard-boiled egg or a sorb-apple! Emilio was not half of a complete man, nor was she half of a whole woman. And if they kissed and fused with such passion, it wasn't out of a desire to regain their lost unity, but on the contrary to magnify their difference. Emilio's sex placed her at a great distance from herself.

Lorna recalled their good-byes at the airport in Rome. Would she ever see him again? The first night they were together once more, right after he'd made love to her without undressing her, he'd pronounced a barely comprehensible speech that was morbidly ambiguous and from which she was still reeling: in addition to the duly noted absence of consciousness, the lack of brain reflexes, and the inability to breathe on one's own, a person cannot be declared dead until an arteriography and two encephalograms are performed, confirming the irrevocable ceasing of all brain function. Lorna was often stunned by the willful perversity of the best-intentioned people when it came to vital issues such as a couple's breakup or a violent death. Because Emilio's words were tinged with jealousy, they frightened her, especially today because of what his account about brain death could mean after her two quick visits to what remained of Cédric in a protected wing of the Rult-Milleur château.

The establishment had been converted into a prestigious hospital by the branch of an insurance group that managed a chain of hospitals in Switzerland and elsewhere in Europe, and was covertly dependent on the M.A.W. Trust. The pharmaceutical industry had the financial means to set up a hospital and donate to charity. While Lorna was contemplating the wintry desolation of the grounds, an employee of the hotel wing of the château called to her. Lorna shivered, her mind wandering, and almost apologized for her tears, which seemed to blend into the mist on the windows. The staff's kindness to her, oddly overplayed, only increased her uneasiness. But she had to go to Geneva for a meeting that worried her even more. During these restless days and nights near the poor dormant head of the only man she had truly loved until now, all her guilt had melted away, replaced by an icy terror. Nothing was actually her fault, unless one believed in some magical spirit. Love could not be a pact with the devil or a contract of possession. Besides, the multidisciplinary functional rehabilitation team in charge of the patient had reassured her regarding the efficacy of the antirejection treatment: Cédric's chances of survival seemed to be taking on heft. As if making a promise, the doctors were now talking about a long period of convalescence, therapies of adaptation to the "graft" once the immunological problems had been resolved, the various treatments related to structural reconstruction, the massage and physical therapy sessions . . .

Still, she felt an overwhelming and uncontrollable oppressiveness inside her. Ever since her terrifying discovery of Cédric's duplicity, an ocean of incomprehension surrounded Lorna, a desert island floating with no anchorage point. And everything that followed, hurricanes and wicked waves, seemed to be one of Neptune's whims.

14.

Lorna went to Cédric's bedside one last time before leaving Rult-Milleur. His body was covered with a sheet and his throat bandaged, so that only the part of him she knew was visible. Yet this face was observing her oddly, as if through different eyes.

"I'll be back in a week or two," she said, without being able to stop gazing at the tiny wrinkles that had appeared on his forehead.

His lips moved around an unpronounceable word before he let out a guttural sound that gradually became clearer.

"I'll be back in a week or two . . ."

"What did you say, Cédric?"

He uttered the words with a studied slowness, as if he were inventing them. His voice had a metallic, almost artificial tone. Lorna placed her hand on the sheet, realizing suddenly that she was touching the other body.

"So you can speak, Cédric! The doctors explained to me that your abilities would return one by one. When I come back, maybe you'll be standing up! We'll be able to walk in the grounds. The landscape in these mountains is sublime . . ."

When the taxi arrived, Lorna left the room in a hurry. Cédric gazed for a long time at the door, as if he could see through it. A bad migraine was pounding his temples. But he wasn't really suffering. It was a sharp pressure, like a hot blade, to which the word *pain* wasn't really suited. The sudden appearance and disappearance of the woman whom he recognized as the one who occupied his physical memory left him in dreamy perplexity. Around him and in him, in what seemed to be him, so many enigmas followed one after the other then abruptly merged together into complete amazement. Through the diamond window, a snow-covered mountain peak altered its shimmer with the passing of the clouds. The sky soon brightened to a deep blue, and the entire mountain was illuminated. Cédric felt a sort of sympathy for this shape of the outside world. With closed eyes, he sought a precise spot of comprehension, but the meaning of things slipped away; there was a misty film covering obstinate presences like that door or that window with its sloped perspective. Which one should he choose for his escape? The sound of a hospital cart rolled through his left ear. Wearing smocks, their hair tucked tightly beneath a hairnet, two women with wide hips came into his room. He recognized them; the one who was pushing the cart wore a carnival mask smile. The other one looked at him fixedly, with a worried pout. They removed the sheet, undid his underthings, and palpated the arms and legs, the chest of this body, the stomach, the crotch, and the perineum.

"What do you feel today?" asked the more experienced woman.

"Your hands," he said.

"That's a start! Now move your right foot, go

ahead. No, not the left, the right. Your right foot corresponds to my left hand, get it? Now raise your left hand, no, not the right. But that's good; you'll get there. The other one now, left or right, it doesn't matter."

The assistant nurse took in, one by one, the inexpressive face, the limp penis, the muscular thighs, the strength of this torso beneath the pale anterior extremity. She couldn't help feeling a kind of religious awe mixed with disgust.

"Miss!" said the physical therapist, annoyed by her assistant's lack of attention.

The assistant drew the sheet back across the naked body. She watched distractedly as her colleague's fingers tapped the patient's jaws to work his facial muscles. Like all the caregivers assigned to this exclusive hospital wing, she'd been sworn to secrecy. And so far, no one had spilled the beans. Besides the usual clientele, the octagonal tower of the Rult-Milleur château attracted only swarms of starlings from the mountain pastures. In fact, convalescents and terminally ill guests did not have access to this high-security wing reserved for celebrities or special cases.

"Your responsiveness is improving every day," said the physical therapist. "Soon you'll be able to move about with a walker."

Cédric exchanged a long look with each of the two women who were about to leave the premises. He found them to be droll, almost comical, especially the nurse with the round eyes of a night bird. For all of them, the uncertainty regarding the consequences and the outcome of this difficult adventure made any communication moot. He was about to be transported in a wheelchair to the office of a certain Hans Morcelet, the psychiatrist in charge of giving him back the use of his mind and his words. Cédric let himself be conveyed like a sack, his head floating above a numb, imprecise sensation composed of shooting pains and twitches.

When he found himself alone again, Cédric let out a childlike moan. The images inside his skull had lost all three-dimensionality; at times they faded away, transparent, almost abstract because they were detached from any stable meaning. When would he find the strength to pull himself out of this gangue that had no defined limits? From time to time, when he least expected it, he would experience a dreadful dizziness: there was no longer anything below him or at the end of him besides an immense suffering similar to the vanished memory of gestures and caresses. He fell spinning into the abyss of an unknown anatomy; he was going to be crushed against a tile floor of oblivion, falling so deeply—but into what grave? His entire being was torn apart; he was a great void lacerated on the inside; molten lead permeated him all the way to the tip of his heart. Cédric felt something like a quiet determination in the pit of his stomach. If body and soul were the same substance, what would remain of him?

15.

Adversity rarely misses an opportunity to frustrate fate. Georgio Cadavero had become the darling of scholarly journals and television shows, had received heaps of praise, almost an equal amount of scathing criticism, and a few death threats. The calls for help from families in distress, the reservations expressed by eminent theologians, the debates regarding the seat of the soul, genetic paternity, or bioethical matters, and protests from groups against euthanasia all participated in the media hullaballoo; the climate was one of noxious fascination in which hopes for survival mingled with castration fantasies. Former patients who considered themselves to have been ill-served because they'd been deprived of glory and the relatives of desperate cases attacked either Cadavero's competence or his integrity. He was, for example, questioned about one too many operations he'd performed on an octogenarian in a coma who had suffered a brain hemorrhage. His insurance managed to settle that lawsuit out of court, but other defamatory matters from his past tainted his accountability and his honor to greater or lesser degrees. The media constantly brought up the possibility of transplant tourism, or even of a "transplant trade," comparable to the slave trade. Thanks to Jean Dausset's well-known research on tissue compatibility, which enabled the immune system's reactions to be controlled, transplants had become globalized, without cultural or ethnic borders, and with the relatively overt support of governments. Whether he was despised or venerated, Cadavero had quickly become a sort of messiah of the ancient longing for eternal life. The least worthy of his contemporaries, phantoms of their former selves, half-robotized and overmedicated, did not want to believe they would die. To them, death was nothing but a virus to be neutralized, a programming error. These precarious passengers of life could not imagine that their synaptic fields were fragile and fleeting, despite their boundless wealth. Even the notion of immortality is subject to cellular corrosion! One becomes human by losing a part of one's defenses, by fighting tooth and nail against the angel of death; experience had taught him this and he'd discussed it abundantly in his work. A world without humanity does not exist, or if it does, it does so only at the nethermost regions of a cadaverous dream.

Nonetheless, an old, senile autocrat from the Balkans, a Russian oligarch in the terminal phase of carcinoma, quadriplegics offering themselves as guinea pigs, and a horde of wealthy impotent men had inquired about Cadavero's services with the aim of changing bodies as fast as possible, by any means. The newspapers were teeming with speculations and dreams. Males unhappy with their gender thought it would at last be possible to adopt a female body in the most intimate way, and women didn't hesitate to visualize taking on some permanent virility. One woman was coveting the body of an adored brother who was brain dead. An old Texas businessman with grand political ambitions suggested giving lifetime terms of office to future Abraham Lincolns or John F. Kennedys, whether they had been assassinated or not, renewing their terms for all eternity to the glory of the nation. Couldn't we in fact imagine a world divided between simple mortals and immortal geniuses in the near future? In this scenario, the heads of Albert Einstein and Nelson Mandela could have enriched and guided successive generations ad libitum. Dependable witnesses to History would thereby be preserved. Each country would have its immortal elites, like fetishized minotaurs onto which one would transplant young, healthy, vigorous, detachable bodies every ten or twenty years. All this boastful blather had an effect on the critics of these hypothetical fairy tales who then, with equal confidence, expressed alarm at the idea of a new generation of Führers capable of wreaking havoc for a thousand years, or an anemic society stockpiling on one side the refrigerated heads of those laying claim to immortality and on the other the bodies of donors with their digitized pedigrees, kept in medically induced comas.

It wasn't long before Cadavero's exploit became subject to doubts: fifty-three days after the operation, only a few photos and videos had been released in response to the uninterrupted flow of commentaries. The world wanted to see the miracle man from head to toe, preferably half naked and leaping in the air. Who could prove that this dervish with a scalpel, part fakir and part magician, had not created out of whole cloth this tallest of tall tales? Sooner or later people were bound to say that after five or six weeks the "soul had departed" from the man-with-another-man's-heart but that no matter what, the whole thing represented considerable progress for science. Although Cadavero was aware of the harm these outpourings were causing him, he was still obliged to respect his schedule and hop a plane to Geneva. His sponsor, the CEO of M.A.W., wanted him there for financial and insurance reasons. As a result, Cadavero was planning a visit to the hospital in the Rult-

Milleur château. It would be his third visit since responsibility for his patient had been transferred to his Swiss colleagues. Cadavero had been assured that the patient, whose immune system was functioning for now and who had come out of a worrisome asthenia, had regained a bit of mobility. The surgeon could at last show visual proof of his feat to the media mob. This would be the premiere of Cédric Allyn-Weberson in his starring role as medicine's miracle man.

16.

Heavy snowfalls obliterated the countryside between Mount Dou, hardly distinguishable from the leaden sky, and the Isangrin Pass, which was now inaccessible. The winding road that led to the Rult-Milleur domain was continually covered by new snowfall, and two snowplows were used to keep the route clear. But the helipad near the tower allowed one to bypass the occasional road closings, and the whirring of helicopter blades accompanied for part of the day the unfamiliar din of the plows.

Looking out through the bay windows at the desolate spectacle, Cédric was listening to Dr. Morcelet's monotonous voice enumerating once again the obstacles to a robust rehab.

"Your father's office has given the orders," he droned on. "When you have regained your executive functions, you can cater to any of Dr. Cadavero's whims. What happened yesterday is beyond belief. It would be terribly detrimental to have you destabilized by all this chaos . . ."

The psychiatrist's darkened face, silhouetted against the sun, stood out against the background of snow-covered cliffs. "All this chaos!" he repeated. The press conference organized the previous day in the château theater had indeed taken the institution's management by surprise. Dr. Cadavero seemed to hold all the power, and it wasn't until journalists from Radiotelevisione Italiana disembarked from helicopter shuttles that a wave of panic went through the hospital administration. Cédric remained confused after what had felt like a hostage taking; it was as if he'd been a contestant in a game show that had morphed into a pre-indictment interrogation. Then the whole crowd got back on the helicopters and headed to Piedmont with the illustrious neurosurgeon. And as if the authorities in Geneva had ordered them, avalanches of snow fell during the night, seemingly to prevent any repeat offense.

"You've become a public figure," sighed Dr. Morcelet.

Cédric avoided eye contact with the psychiatrist. He didn't understand what such a statement was supposed to mean to him. Never again could he embody any sort of figure whatsoever. Something essential—he didn't know quite what—was lacking from this unique instance of being alive thanks to someone else's anatomy. He also avoided looking at those hands (supposedly his) lying flat on the flaps of his bathrobe. The only part of him he dared examine, at times with nightmarish apprehension, was his face. He still accepted this bodily part as if it belonged to him, although suspicious grimaces appeared on it, with an indefinable expression in the gaze and mysterious coloring on the temples and chin. His head—and indeed it was his—seemed balanced precariously on the spine of some unlikely pachyderm. The psychiatrist, thinking he was reassuring Cédric, attributed these bad spells to the considerable posttraumatic effects of the transplant, which were accompanied by a disturbance of visual messages, by a likely dysfunction of the internal ear, by a variety of coenesthetic mirages, and, last but not least, by problems of posture.

"Your most recent exams don't show any nerve damage. Rest assured, you will wind up adapting to feeling on intimate terms with your new body, and by fully adopting its center of gravity."

As he uttered these words, Dr. Morcelet felt his throat contract slightly. The freak-show phenomenon before him did not correspond to any model that neuroscience had conceived. The dissociative problems from which this sad hybrid was suffering were to be expected under the circumstances: depersonalization, selective amnesia, and other symptoms to which bizarre interferences were added. The functional rehabilitation program had in fact foreseen that Cédric would have difficulty accepting his new unity: how could a human head weighing a few pounds—supposing that it had retained all its cognitive functions—adapt smoothly to the intrusion of this enormous graft, a beheaded stranger? Morcelet deemed that the notorious multiple personality disorder so dear to Americans, but absent from the statistical books of mental health problems, would be apt in the case of this new clinical example. He coughed, one hand in front of his mouth.

"But do the pains in your body lessen after the electric stimulation sessions?"

Cédric shrugged without moving at all above the axis vertebra. The core of pain that estranged him from all known sensations, whether on standby or in sleep mode, sometimes at the slightest touch, had nothing in common with some vague "psycho-physiological" manifestations. It wasn't a question of hallucinosis, or else the "phantom" in him inhabited him completely.

"It's as if I were being asked to report . . ."

"What do you mean exactly?"

"It's as if I were a dead man occupying the place of a living man."

With pins and needles in his legs, the psychiatrist hesitated for a few seconds, searching for the right words. The sensation of a limb or a phantom organ spread over the whole body could not be so terrible because there were no damaged nerve endings like those in a residual limb; unless the transplanted body had taken over, and the trauma had been transmitted through the donor's spinal cord?

"What do you feel in your cervical spine?"

"Do you mean my scar? At times, it feels like a boa is swallowing a rhinoceros."

On the way back to his room, with a nurse at his elbow as he leaned on a walker, Cédric perplexedly repeated the therapist's last words: "If you can use metaphors for your pain, it's a sign that it already hurts less!"

17.

A glacial cold had transformed the thick snow into ice. Everywhere statues of stalactites appeared and spectral figures could be glimpsed through the trees, the highway equipment, or the masts of the many sailboats in the harbor between the municipalities of Coppet and Versoix, where a literary grande dame had once lived. Partially frozen near the shore, Lake Geneva sparkled like a steel blade beneath the blue sky. From the windows of the manor, you could make out the western part of Geneva on the other side of the bridge, and the foothills of the Jura glimmered with starlight in the dawn.

Lorna stared at these austere sights from the dreamy distance that insomnia leaves in its wake. The previous night, she'd become more convinced of her need to get away, at least for a time. After the months she had taken off from work, her news agency was now offering her a trip to Arabia Felix. Tribal insurrections had spread to the entire region, reigniting the most muddled of civil wars among the Arab Spring demonstrators in Sana'a: Islamist rebels, Shiite minority fighters, and government troops supported by Saudi Arabia. The infamous risks of the job had surprisingly curative powers against depression. She recalled having met Cédric at a cocktail party at his magazine's headquarters five years earlier, when she'd returned from Baghdad. When he learned of the massacre in the Syrian Catholic church in Baghdad from which she'd just escaped, Cédric practically apologized for being an armchair journalist. Still, by attacking major corporations, he was in fact perhaps more vulnerable than she was. Lawsuits, intimidations, blackmail, and physical assaults were part and parcel of his professional life.

The previous day, alone with Cédric's father in an enormous living room the size of a reception hall in a Swiss bank, Lorna couldn't help inquiring somewhat obliquely about the irreparable disagreement between the businessman and his son, and the probably not inconsistent motives for Morice's so distant yet so substantial aid. An old man with gray eyes and a transparent smile on his thin face, Morice Allyn-Weberson had asked her to stay for dinner after their early afternoon interview as the snow fell in large, foamy waves on Lake Geneva.

"Why did Cédric break all ties with his family? Is it because of your business activities?"

The head of the M.A.W. laboratories nodded distraughtly.

"Most probably. You've read his work; he accuses us of the worst evils . . ."

"Is he wrong?" Lorna asked candidly, keeping one eye on the strange butler who served and then cleared up with mechanical slowness.

"For Cédric, the entire pharmaceutical industry is an international criminal organization responsible for the pathological alienation of just about all the world's peoples with the heinous complicity of governments and public health services! According to this line of thought, I, who take a good dozen medications every day, must logically be a victim of my own laboratories . . ."

Lorna smiled at this rather forced riposte. Cédric had not worn kid gloves to denounce the falsified favorable studies, the bribing of politicians and scientific experts, the pharmacists' seminars in the Maldives or the Seychelles, the artificial creation of morbid symptoms or side effects that then required new drug dependencies, the testing of previously untested and often toxic molecules on impoverished people in Africa and Latin America.

"I see you're smiling," the billionaire said. "Yet I am merely a cog in the machine; my company depends on, but does not control, an industrial holding company whose sole aim is to expand its interests. It is a brain without a soul, I grant you. But you cannot fight an economic machine, you know, whether you're an economist, a rabble-rouser, or a financier. Unlike Voltaire's famous watch, this huge crazy clock with its millions of watch hands does not really have a watchmaker . . ."

From the bay windows overlooking the lake, Lorna, slightly dazzled, was scrutinizing the ice figures on the shore and deep within the property grounds. One of those figures, near a fountain that had become a mirror, must have been an actual statue beneath the stalactites. With such a sea of ice, her departure for Rome later that morning seemed unlikely, to say the least. Did she really have such a great desire to see Emilio again? She would change her ticket and take a nonstop flight to Yemen from the Geneva airport after spending a comatose night at the hotel.

The previous day Morice Allyn-Weberson had been eager to offer her a photograph of Cédric at twenty. In a bathing suit on the beach, he was glowing with youth and the fragile harmony between a body and soul faced with life's mysteries. Lorna had sensed that this curious gift would be followed by some revelation. The businessman had practically blessed her for having contacted him the day after the accident and come to visit him in Geneva three months later despite her misgivings.

"Cédric is my only child," he confided. "He hates me but he is my son. I've continued to love him from afar ever since he broke off all contact with me after his mother's tragic death. Perhaps he didn't tell you that she threw herself out a window in front of me? Cédric didn't believe it was a suicide. When you're twelve years old, how can you believe your mother would kill herself? Because she'd attempted to hang herself a few days earlier, I wasn't really a suspect. But Cédric turned against me, and since then we've hardly exchanged a single word! After he finished his studies at an elite boarding school, he ran away several times before disappearing completely. It didn't take me long to track him down. Do you think I didn't know his alias? In a way, I've never left him. I've followed his escapades without his knowledge. All his movements were communicated to me, with the exception of the last one, on the sailboat. I'm angry with you, Lorna. Because of your whim, I was unable to save him."

Lorna interrupted him forcefully: how could he have prevented a winch from falling accidentally? The old man preserved his somewhat haughty, if not contemptuous, affability.

"You must know that money is power and provides a number of opportunities. But what happened is an insurmountable tragedy: my son no longer has his original body; he is no longer genetically my son. Do you understand? If he has children with you, they'll have the other man's genes!"

Lorna's eyes widened with fear at the monstrousness of such reasoning. Clearly the bourgeoisie placed heredity among its vital interests, on a par with its need for control. At that moment, overcome with nausea, she excused herself and went back to her room to vomit up her entire meal. As soon as she lay down in the half-light of the ice and the full moon, she made every effort to forget. But Cédric's naked body slid beneath her sheets and she thought she'd moaned for a long time either from fright or from pleasure without betraying for a moment the silence of her dream.

The following day, the sight of all those convulsed statues throughout the countryside was reminiscent of moraines that had been expelled from the estuary of a glacier. The bizarre man with his robotic movements had carried down Lorna's luggage. As she was leaving, when a car with notched wheels pulled up, Morice Allyn-Weberson wanted to say good-bye at the door to this daughter-in-law who had been sent from heaven. He knew just about everything about her; his investigators had even informed him about her sexual escapades and her absurd taste for hardship and danger. He did not dislike her, despite her misgivings about him. A woman who puts her life at risk like that could not be greedy; outside of business, he only cared for such selfless people.

"Farewell, Lorna. Come back to see me when you get a chance. I have faith in you. I know you won't abandon my son, so what can I say to you? Cédric despises me but that doesn't matter. Nonetheless, I'm going to tell you a secret: his real body, his poor, broken, and amputated body is lying in the family vault, with his mother . . ."

Horrified by the old man's lunacy, Lorna exclaimed: "If your son were to die from immune rejection or something else, what would you do with him?"

"I'd place his head in there too!" he answered calmly. "Yes, his real body is waiting for him in a decay-proof coffin. A man such as myself can obtain any authorization he wants. I would place his head in there and have his name engraved next to mine. Can you imagine for a second that I would be able to outlive him? In fact, I will probably die before he does. If that happens, take good care of him; you obviously love him. Cédric is my sole successor in this world, you understand? And I don't trust anyone, especially not my associates. And I'm going to tell you one more secret, a hypothesis in fact, a plausible suspicion, but you have to swear on my son's head that you will never, ever repeat it . . ."

18.

Situated on a cliff overhanging the Adriatic Sea, in the middle of a wood in the province of Trieste, Dr. Emil Schoeler's establishment was a refuge for patients looking for peace and quiet. It was both a hospital and a convalescent center, where celebrities in need of anonymity and people under various threats were treated in a discreet and extremely secure environment. Following the televised conference at the Rult-Milleur château that had exposed Cédric to the public in order to gratify the egos of his surgeons, the only way for him to escape the permanent siege of busybodies and journalists was to get away from there as quickly as possible. As his guardian, Dr. Servil had tended to every detail. The mission of that mediator from Geneva was to never have direct contact with the patient and to oversee the quality of care at each of his visits. The facilities offered to the son of a magnate of the pharmaceutical industry should be a matter of course, without ostentation but with all the efficiency of constant and complete aid of all kinds.

Within the best care system imaginable, Cédric very naturally became accustomed to this level of comfort. Once you lose any hope of recognizing yourself in space, the world around you resembles time wasted. With the Adriatic in front of him, in his scenic solitude surrounded by craggy forests and dark mountains, the grounds, with their huge oaks, were the ideal space for a kind of episodic, and sometimes spasmodic, resurrection that caused him as much painful fear as instinctive surprise in the midst of birdsong and branches swaying in the sea breeze. Every morning an intact sun followed without the slightest veil of mist the most resplendent night sky. Trailed from a distance by a nurse, he was allowed to wander at his own pace along the shaded alleys. Cédric had the impression he was walking on a carpet of cicadas and bees, so much did his eyes respond by flashes and flickers to the sounds all around him. He had trouble delineating the boundaries of his five senses; summer colors tasted of sap and sounds warmed his skin; scents even invaded his ears and eyes. During a recent consultation, Dr. Schoeler, a distinguished neurologist, thought he was reassuring Cédric in describing to him a probable disorder in the connections of millions of spinal cord fibers—some of which were still being reconstituted—and the delayed impulses linked to the distortions of organ memories.

Cédric indeed was no longer sure of his memories and from time to time came up against an obtuse will that entered him from outside his consciousness. How can you believe in your own past, and even your emotions, when your body is haunted by another's history? Ever since he had come out of the cycle of anesthesia and medically induced comas, his brain seemed detached from reality, as if he were simply experiencing unreliable representations from REM sleep:

a sort of crystalline, luminous, almost abstract dream.

Cédric had just glimpsed his guardian angel through a looped alleyway that wound between the tulip beds. Her hands in the pockets of a light smock, the nurse let him come up to her and then turned halfway to face the man she'd been following a moment ago.

"Oh, such a lovely stroll!" she said once he was near. "Every day you move about more easily . . ."

"You mean I'm only limping with one leg now!"

He stared at her, surprised in the daylight by her bland, touching beauty beneath the white band of her nurse's cap. Was that elusive emotion he felt in the presence of a female located in his brain, or lower down, deep inside the entrails that did not belong to him?

"Do you think I'll be able to go home one day?" he asked, without the slightest memory of a place where he'd lived.

"Certainly," said the nurse, who had been trained to acquiesce to the wishes of the clientele. "As soon as you've regained enough autonomy."

"Physical you mean?"

"Of course. But also when you no longer get dizzy in front of a mirror and when you've agreed to eat in the hospital cafeteria."

"But I eat everything I'm given!"

"And if we didn't give you anything, you wouldn't eat a thing. It's as if we were throwing roses through a circus hoop!"

The young woman was now strolling more slowly next to her protégé. As they walked, the view changed, opening now onto the island-filled sea, now onto the illuminated mountains.

"I'd like to know . . . ," said Cédric in a hesitant voice.

"What is it? I'm listening."

"What am I related to? What do I resemble physically on this earth?"

"A man, it would appear."

"You don't understand! Let's go back in now, this light is piercing my skull!"

During the days that followed, Cédric, aware that he was improving, requested the authorization to go out, to visit Trieste, to go swimming. Wasn't he in fact a free man? The director of the establishment promised to grant all his wishes, but a little later on, after a battery of additional tests. "Transthoracic sonogram, primitive reflex, oculomotor function . . . nothing but the usual," he explained. Cédric would have to content himself with the grounds and its alleyways for another week, but he was obsessed with a recurring idea. Was he not free to make his own choices? Changing bodies did not entail any known type of madness, provided that the brain system was intact. His brain had no lesions, he felt warmth in his limbs, and these now moved at his will—except on some nights when he was affected by the sleep paralysis associated with short periods of hallucination. True, he was still experiencing total alienation; you don't switch bodies the way you do dance partners. He was not psychologically whole. And his relative health was due entirely to a surgical construction. Despite massive doses of medicine, his head could reject the body at any moment. He also knew that the immunosuppressant treatments increased his chances of lymphoma and other cancers. And then, he no longer had any sexual feeling, no libido; this part of him seemed to be extinguished for good. He was particularly preoccupied by the idea that he could no longer be genuinely autonomous. In his state of dependency, he felt incapable of using his reasoning or acting on his own. Freedom of thought had to be immersed in flesh and blood in order not to be an artifice of pure reasoning. Although it occupied a privileged space in the brain, free will had to be the result of a hormonal secretion, at best a localized activity of synapses. The entire body had to be involved in the slightest decision. The thought of leaving, running away as before with Lorna, took on a variety of contours. Was her name really Lorna?

Tormented by a mysterious bewilderment, in the end he conceded that this confused yearning—the only thing that could reassure him that he hadn't been amputated from his inner self—must surely involve his physical and moral independence.

19.

One autumn morning, Cédric awoke with a start and sat up in bed as daylight filtered through the blinds. He must have been dreaming about the woman he loved, but her name escaped him. Had they broken up? Even though he had difficulty imagining her features, he was flooded with infinite sadness at the thought of such a possibility. Anyway, what was he doing alone in this bed, battered by cramps and twinges from head to toe? He folded down the sheet, recalling that he'd gone to bed naked the previous night because he was allergic to the seams on the flannel pajamas he'd found among the various new clothes in the drawers of a dresser. He had never asked himself where they'd come from. His care, the treatments he was given, the impeccable accommodations of the various establishments where he stayed—all of that must have cost a fortune. He observed with growing unease the huge bedroom that had been conceived for optimal comfort, although it came with the discreet presence of a medical surveillance robot no doubt connected to the computers of a host of clinicians. In the left corner, near a window above his bed, between two lamps, video cameras closely monitored his most intimate moments. "Soon you'll no longer even notice them," Dr. Schoeler had told him. "We forget quite quickly any outside intrusion if it's painless."

Not thinking about the cameras, for the first time and without gagging, Cédric examined the territory of the body that spread out beneath his chin. At his request, he'd been able to observe his face in a mirror. Something in his gaze and his expression had changed, yet he'd recognized himself, the way one discovers oneself again in a hotel room after a long journey to the other side of the world. But he did not recognize this body; he'd never experienced anything with it other than passive functions like urinating or defecating, which were no longer really of his doing. It was as if someone were using his presence, this sentient configuration that he couldn't forget. Eating, too, was a challenge for him, but of a different sort. He would chew his food for a longer time before it disappeared into the abyss. Were there two of them sharing a plate of mashed potatoes or an apple? Was he this glutton's taster? Cédric recalled an exchange with his Swiss psychiatrist. Cédric had asked him, as a provocation, why people didn't consider him to be the transplant rather than the body. All that remained of him was a head, and the other man's body that linked him again to his animal life was much more imperious and invasive. "What is unique about every human being is what is contained in a skull," the psychiatrist had responded. "Consciousness, personality." Nevertheless, the vital impulses passed through this heart and these intestines and went back up all the way to the tips of his hair.

He touched the left arm, crossed the fingers, slid them down to the stomach, palpated the penis and the scrotum and, sitting up, continued toward the thighs and calves, then slid back up, this time with both hands, to the chest. He noticed several beauty marks on the torso, like a constellation, and brown hairs on spots that were unusual for him, along with a scar on the groin and several others on a forearm and the thighs, no doubt from vaccinations. The penis under his palm still did not respond. The fact that it might not be able to get erect hardly bothered him; he was incapable of imagining making love to a woman one day with the organ of another man. Even though the proportions were similar to his, the creature on which his head was sitting was more muscular, stronger, more solidly built. The body was impeccable in appearance and must have been a few years younger than Cédric. And certainly it had been in perfect health before winding up in the Emergency Room and inheriting the head of a quadriplegic cuckoo bird.

For the first time since his accident, Cédric shook with the beginning of a laughing fit, but it quickly turned into a sob as he registered the convulsions of this chest that didn't belong to any known life form. Must one be self-aware in order to laugh and bring about the body's mechanisms? His greatest surprise was to see his motor reflexes reacting to his thoughts.

As he was examining every nook and cranny of skin, he noticed a small bluish tattoo on the underside of one arm: three entwined spirals with something resembling a face in the center. This marking scared him somewhat, as if it had been inflicted on him without his knowledge. Then, realizing that his suffering was still raw at the memory of his previous body, kicked out by this resolutely foreign physiognomy that he despaired of appropriating one day, Cédric experienced a sort of tenderness for the tattoo, the whim that had it inscribed, the narcissism it took to choose the design and suffer the pain of the needles.

After a rather clumsy use of the hands as tools to explore all the minuscule bumps and ridges of the skin, he began to examine the hands themselves, palms open, and once more he was frightened at no longer recognizing, after so many years, their oval shape and their boniness. Those hands, thick and hard, didn't resemble his at all. The life line was that of someone who would live to be a hundred; the head line, identical across both palms, would have revealed a positive spirit if one believed in palmistry. Bending and unbending the fingers, he noticed that the middle and ring fingers of the left hand were stiff. In the fleshy part of the right thumb, a scar bore witness to a rather deep wound that must have required several stitches. The fingernails were rounded, surprisingly translucent, with light pink half-moons. Each time a nurse had clipped them for him, he was reminded of the fact that nails and hair continue to grow after death. Are there manicurists for the dead, hairdressers for corpses? All the peculiarity of his new nature was contained in the collar of flesh and slightly indurated skin at his throat and neck. From time to time he would graze it with his fingertips, thinking that this huge scar alone belonged to both body and head, the border of two broken lives. Why had they not grafted, as a counterpoint, the debrained skull of his donor onto his destroyed body? Perhaps such a monster could—in solidarity—at least have attested to their previous lives.

"*Signor* Cédric!" cried the nurse gaily, as she came in to give him some medicine.

"Are you shocked that he's naked?" Cédric answered almost spontaneously.

"So, you're talking about yourself in the third person now?"

Cédric was silent while the nurse strapped his arm. He was thinking that children and monarchs speak of themselves in this way, as if in someone else's stead. In Italian, it was a grammatical form of politeness. Surely there must have been a third person somewhere.

20.

From a first-class trauma center to a recovery and rehabilitation establishment, between yet another operation and the threat of a sudden increase in antibody levels, Cédric—the problematic miracle man—had to endure several more months of the ups and downs of his transplant surgery. He was surprised in an obscure, apathetic way at the strange moral abandonment in which he had been confined. Every now and again a female voice emitted words of encouragement and affection over the phone, but he had difficulty placing it. Was it his girlfriend's? He seemed to recall that she had broken up with him once upon a time. Then the image of a large sailboat cleaving through steel-colored waters came cruelly back to him. Still under the impersonal guardianship of Dr. Servil and the maniacal attention of other physicians for whom every hour he survived was worth a fortune, he began to think that his willpower was possibly being slowly annihilated. At this point he was allowed to take so-called "comfort" drugs whenever he liked, and he swore to himself that he would discreetly eliminate all those liable to cause any biochemical imbalance. He knew that this decision had only been made once his metabolism had evolved. His sense of individuality was restored little by little with the gradual recovery of a memory that until then had been purely cerebral, without any real object. His consciousness, in regaining some authority over his sensations as they rose through his internal organs and his nerve endings, seemed to have to extricate itself from a dreamlike tenuousness that had pushed it to the side, in a bubble of unconsciousness, without a thought for the outside world. It was as if, as he was slowly freed from a mighty inhibition of a medicated sort, the road to his emancipation was taking shape: the need to understand, a desire for freedom, the intention to escape the dubious constraints of his environment. As his mind became clearer, he couldn't help but grasp his condition as a dependent guinea pig, a unique phenomenon sequestered by medical authorities. Even if it were a privileged one, when would this institutionalized condition end?

With this return to lucidity, it soon became obvious to him that his survival had been financed at considerable cost. One didn't change bodies without having a fortune at one's disposal, unless one was a laboratory animal or a subject of a covert experiment who soon wound up in a morgue. He had been chosen for this opening night, with the elites of science in the box seats and public opinion in the orchestra seats.

One January morning, for the first time Cédric felt warmth in his loins and a sort of quivering. With a hesitant finger, and the painful impression of committing an indecent act, he touched a penile tumescence. Soon there was a full erection. He recalled that on a tortured body—hanged or strangled—such an erection pointed to imminent death. Nevertheless, he manipulated this penis for a long time, as if to tame it; even if one hadn't undergone an almost total transplant, the most autonomous, almost uncontrollable part of the body of any ordinary man was his penis. The size of this penis was intriguing to Cédric's touch, its shape a raised arc: one more absurdity that in the end made him moan in pain. He was resentful when he thought of that other man with his lovely smooth muscles who, decapitated and transplanted onto a luckier man, had nonetheless kept for himself alone, for his headless body, all his attributes, like a starfish or the immortal jellyfish. Would Cédric regain his pleasure as a parasite, a kind of sea lamprey clinging to this pelagic body? Even if he managed to accept his transplant, the promised symbiosis with his unknown host seemed to him completely repulsive and unnatural. What was he to do with this hybrid, double reality now? He had the irrepressible feeling of a duality of body and mind, a sense of a monstrous coexistence. This erect penis in no way replaced his urogenital tract; it was simply superimposed on dormant former functions. And that heart in the middle of the ribs beat to a different rhythm from the one in the temporal lobes of his brain. Those too-wide hands, so idle, had once adapted to desires of which he remained ignorant. They had experienced embraces, caresses; perhaps they had even killed. All of a sudden Cédric was overwhelmed by the despair of a searing sense of exile from and actual suffering for his broken body, the one that had most likely been incinerated with the other man's head. If he were to survive, would Cédric perpetually have to endure the torments of that ghost?

The telephone rang, reminding him that he was supposed to go out with his assigned nurse, a kind of mischievous governess; nevertheless, he answered after the second ring.

"Cédric," he heard. "Is that you? I'm back. Don't ask me to explain anything. After Yemen, after what I've seen and experienced, I had to get away. Don't ask me anything, I can't stop thinking of you, and I've never stopped loving you . . ."

21.

The climate of civil war just about everywhere in the world, the indiscriminate terrorist attacks, and the increased police surveillance have not spared any European capital, but Paris seems to have regained its state of blissful relaxation with the first days of summer. The spring rains, which were torrential until mid-June, have ceded to beautiful sunshine. Can one imagine light without the sun? As Cédric Erg wakes up and his gaze turns to the reflections moving across his windows, he remembers having read somewhere in Nerval something like *the daylight of dreams has no sun.* Since he returned to Paris and rue du Regard, he has begun to dream again, and these dreams, luminous, frighten him by the absence of the celestial body and even more by the lack of awareness he has of them. Can one in fact speak about awareness in a dream?

A clock somewhere in the apartment building, probably right upstairs from him, clangs out six o'clock with the hoarse sound of old metal springs. The warmth of a thigh reminds him of a mysterious change in peripheral sensations. Between what is not really him and this woman under the sheets, a phenomenon of extreme gentleness is diffused all the way to the depths of his eyeballs, behind his eyes, in an unlocatable point of his brain. Lorna glides her warm hand across the pectoral muscles, follows with her fingertips the outline of the abdominal muscles, and slides a palm in the hairy hollow of the groin, grasping an already erect penis. While she takes pains to masturbate it in a blind back-and-forth movement, novel images appear to him, along with old memories of when Lorna and he barely knew each other. Relationships begin in the crudest way, by an instinct of the flesh, as if the boundaries of the senses had to be crossed at all costs. Cédric cannot help comparing the way people have of touching each other and taking each other at the start, in a mixture of abandon and unease, with what he is experiencing today, between him and him, him and the other man. Getting used to this new body after so much time seems like an appropriation of a sexual kind, a disturbing usurpation, a rape almost. And Lorna's excitement adds to his confusion. The last straw is the jealous impulse that overtakes him when he sees her writhing on top of him. She has straddled him and is moaning without for a moment looking him in the eye, given over entirely to this masculine body, her fingers grabbing onto its hips. He feels betrayed and abused at the very spot of his pleasure. No longer anything but a head resting on a narrow structure of bones, how can he identify with the other man, with his desirable body?

"I love when you let me take control!" whispers Lorna. "Oh, I'm about to come with you . . ."

Now she is slumped over, her face on the heart. Her lips pull playfully at the hairs around the left nipple. Not once did she kiss or touch his face, occupied only with the muscular and quivering body. What can one do with just a head? Was his own feeling at the moment of orgasm merely the idea of orgasm? Lorna's splendid head of hair is rolled in electric rings, a python of coolness that surrounds her. She has pulled back a little, her head still bent forward.

"I'm so happy we're together again," she says in her normal voice. "Even if we'll have to live differently. Do you agree?"

"It's already a fact that we're breaking up."

"I don't want to lose you, Cédric. We'll meet again from time to time at your place or somewhere else—whatever you want."

She was silent for a moment, fascinated as she noticed in the light the scar on his neck.

"I came," she says, turning her eyes away. "What about you? Did you like it?"

He thinks for a moment about the incongruity of her question.

"Yes. Making love sticks the pieces back together, everything moves from the sex to the brain, or the opposite. You loved me better and much less, before . . ."

"Better and less well? What do you mean?"

She asks this in a neutral voice that expects no response. Her beautiful heavy breasts roll upon each other as she raises her head, her chin on her fist. Two gold bracelets jingle as they slide from her wrist to the muscles tightened around her elbow. She flinches when she sees a bluish shadow on her lover's arm.

"A tattoo!" she cries. "It's a triskelion, a Celtic symbol. The three legs represent the sun's movement. Or the three worlds, those of the spirits, the living, and the dead . . ."

He notices her expression of intense curiosity with its traces of desire, almost covetousness, as well as a kind of shocked repugnance. Embarrassed at having been caught out, Lorna looks him in the eye in spite of herself and bites her lips, shivering at the sight of this head that she no longer really recognizes. He hasn't changed, at least his face hasn't, with the exception of a few gray hairs around his temples and a core of distraught sorrow in his eyes, but this body that fans her desire no longer coincides with the face; it moves and reacts differently, its peppery scent excites her all the way to the small of her back. Is it possible to desire a stranger with astonishment, in the most conjoined intimacy? In Kobane, having taken refuge on the roof of her hotel with a colleague from a German magazine, she witnessed the public beheading of a young rebel by a squad armed with machine guns and rocket-propelled grenades. The head had fallen in the dust drizzled with purple vomit while the kneeling body had refrained from collapsing for a moment, as if some reflex stemming from pride had tensed its muscles. Then the assistant to the executioner, who'd been busy cleaning his ax, grabbed the bloody, dust-covered head by the hair and shoved it into a garbage bag while at the same time the shoulders of the dead body fell to the ground in a macabre prostration. Wherever she went, this scene haunted her, preventing her from seeing Cédric for a very long time. In a profession where the sight of atrocities becomes ordinary, some circumstances can lead to madness. Cédric's head had rolled night after night in the bright glare and dust of a dream, while the body of the tortured man, wrists tied, had slumped with the same hideous slowness.

Lorna absent-mindedly skims the tattoo with her index finger.

As he feels her touch, Cédric lets out a short, hollow laugh.

"Do you think he was Irish? The triskelion belongs to Irish folklore, doesn't it? Like the harp and the Celtic cross."

Lorna swiftly removes her hand and sits up in bed.

"It's late!" she says. "I've got a meeting at the office . . ."

As she searches for her scattered clothes, she spins around in the early morning light. Her breasts and supple hips move beneath the dark cascade of her hair. Her nudity has the splendor of a marble Venus made of one slab. Her perfection lacks nothing, not even the feet and hands of Aphrodite of Knidos. Cédric watches her go off toward the bathroom, her buttocks swaying above her long thighs. His desire overcomes him from a distance, unattached to the body, from unfathomable depths. Once again while she disappears from view, he experiences a painful, fierce kind of stump removal, a ghostly feeling in the lost regions of himself. Is his mind undergoing, symmetrically, the repercussions of an absurd surgical procedure, to the extent of becoming someone else in turn?

Suffering from a migraine, with the image of clouds sinking into a mountain lake in his head, he falls asleep at the edge of a dream. Someone is threatening to kill him; he has just opened a multitude of anonymous letters in the shape of bird skulls quickly crushed in the hollow of a fist and thrown in the trash. As he leaves the editorial offices of the magazine, swarms of starlings fly out of the sewers, but he pays no attention to them. Dusk spreads out across the birds. Unhappy with his day, he dives into the restless, preholiday crowd. Someone shoves him violently with a shoulder for no reason. He absorbs the impact and, out of breath, continues on his way. Lorna is expecting him for dinner. His good mood returns at the mere thought of this. In a few strides he is in front of her building. Ignoring the elevator, he climbs up the darkened staircase. Remarkably beautiful, like an actress when the curtain falls, Lorna greets him in an evening gown. Her horrified look forces him to explain himself. But she doesn't want to hear it; she's waving her arms and is about to scream. Suddenly he realizes that she doesn't recognize him. "But it's me, Cédric Erg, it's me!" He tries to make her hear him. But as he says these words, he glimpses a stranger's face in the big hall mirror and then recalls being shoved. How can he convince Lorna that he is himself, that someone simply stole his appearance in a moment in a crowd? Panicked by the loud cries of a thousand starlings, he promises to catch the thief and flees—without the hope of ever returning—down the dark staircase where every step has the look and feel of a cetacean vertebra.

22.

The Luxembourg Garden in the spring, when the stained-glass light moves through the trees, allows one to daydream about one's most vivid memories. For a few days Cédric felt himself coming alive again through his earliest recollections. The purest sensations from his childhood, which continually returned to him intact between ordeals, revitalized everything with an air of novelty. He'd spent the past weeks taking multiple psycho-technical exams, undergoing neuropsychological assessments and other biological tests amid an army of leading medical experts from France, Italy, and elsewhere. In his case, there were countless risk factors. He owed entirely to Lorna the fact that he'd managed to escape compulsory quarantine after several months of functional rehabilitation and convalescence. An excellent investigative journalist, she'd used the International Covenant on Civil and Political Rights to force his affable jailers to give him back his freedom. Because he was not insane, a drug addict, an alcoholic, or homeless, nor was he likely to spread a contagious disease, there were no grounds for hospitalization without consent, and Lorna, despite warnings and intimidations, did not have to go to court.

Cédric had returned with a sort of sorrowful pleasure to his apartment on rue du Regard, to his books, and to his old habits, as if they were a precious part of him. When he opened his closets, he was truly dismayed to discover that his shoes no longer fit. His former ways, however, gradually brought him back some peace of mind. Still, the bathroom mirror never failed to reveal to him what a medical monster he'd become. He was alive through some miracle. In this hallowed hour of late morning in the Luxembourg Garden, with his relative autonomy, it seemed to him that his survival was like a new dawn at the mouth of a river. Whatever happened now could never be worse than the tragedy he'd already experienced. Why shouldn't he forsake ordinary illusions, starting with the need to be seductive, and his superfluous desires, his opinions, his hope? The lovely light of the moment, the sunlight dappling the leaves and the faces of students who laughed as they strolled about should be fully sufficient for his relative well-being. Though he had lost everything when he'd lost his body—his emotional bearings and the conventional methods of relating to others—he still had the ability to go about freely or to end it all. He remembered having accepted when he was in a semi-conscious state the idea of the transplant, thinking that if he didn't die right away, at least the operation would offer him sufficient mobility to commit suicide. But the taste for life is as tenacious as a tick. Although, fiber after fiber, his spinal cord recovery was still imperfect, after a few months it had allowed him to regain his mobility in space, so that now he could wander equipment-free among the statues and chestnut trees of the Garden. Of course he still hobbled slightly, and stiffness and tics made him resemble a disjointed marionette, while mortal panic at the slightest cold prevented him from mixing with crowds or taking public transportation; nonetheless, he had a sense of rebirth once he was out in the fresh air. He needed to forget his private impotence and the cruelty of both being and not being himself; more than anything, he needed to forget the faceless question that had obsessed him night and day since his abetted breakout from Dr. Schoeler's hospital. The body he inhabited had once had a genetic and social identity. Anonymous voices sometimes whispered to him through the abyss of his brain. They murmured from deep within his organs. It was a siren song at the edges of unknown reefs, as if he should let himself be carried off by this transplanted body and abandon himself to the outrageous question that this body, impossible to subjugate, was repeatedly asking as it beat on its intestinal walls to the rhythm of his heart: Who am I? Once he was outside, however, walking unsteadily among the statues and trees, he forgot his bodily prison and all the impediments of his implausible handicap.

His solitude, regained after all the media hounding and the requirements of his rehab, paradoxically opened new horizons for him: once again he could fantasize freely in the May sun, beneath the flowers of a handkerchief tree or a red buckeye tree, even though he was followed everywhere he went. None of the movements around him escaped his sight, whether the wake of a child's sailboat in the octagonal basin or the figure of a bodyguard assigned to watch over him behind the rows of lindens. He had developed rare brain activity, a hypersensitivity not far from hallucination. Indeed his neurologists had warned him about the probability of mental disturbances: not only was there the trauma of the transplant, but his brain stem had also been connected de facto with another organic and reflex memory, heterogeneous energies, a peripheral nervous system that was perhaps inassimilable, and that "second brain," the gut, whose spectrum of influence we still do not know. What was happening to Cédric was a chance empowerment, a lasting synchronicity between two independent series, a relation of uncertainty.

Without his knowledge and without straining the spine, Cédric shrugged the phantom shoulders of his former body. A flock of pigeons came plunging down at his feet with the sound of whistling sabers. A woman exasperated by her children stared at him for some time. Beneath his disguise, did she recognize the man with the severed head from the tabloids? Cédric went to limp around the octagonal basin where the little sailboats with their colored hulls were bobbing. His nurse followed him from a distance, carrying a first-aid kit. All those people on his heels did not prevent him from imagining a life other than this solid-gold lab rat/witness, even if that life had no future. He'd had enough of the interview requests from all over the world, of the more or less delusional threats of kidnapping, enough of harassment by all sorts of maniacs and advances from innkeepers or publishers and, as a result, enough of the security people from the division of temporary missions of the Protection Service. For now he was living incognito in his Paris apartment and was informed of all this buzz around him by everyone in Turin, Geneva, and the rehabilitation center of the Rult-Milleur château, where he was supposedly still residing. He had taken back his assumed identity without whetting his neighbors' curiosity. If Cédric Allyn-Weberson was almost as famous as Neil Armstrong or Yuri Gagarin, the journalist Cédric Erg had long been forgotten. Behind the mask with which he thought he'd been hiding from his father's vigilance, at least now he could disappear from the world. He knew that if he were to flee, he would be hunted down wherever he went, like the thief who'd stolen the blue diamond from the Saudi palace. His goal was not to change his life. He could hardly imagine he would last another year. Yet Cédric would have liked to learn the provenance of the moods that affected him and of all those sensations on which he was now dependent. He was filled with unbearable discomfort, a kind of indignant lack of privacy that some psychiatrists attempted to explain with the words "phase of narcissistic appropriation with homosexual components." Bullshit! He simply felt a pain in his emptiness and was terribly ashamed. "Who told you that you were naked?" his creator asks Adam. Before Cédric's accident, when the question of his physical completeness never had reason to arise, his nakedness belonged to him alone, without his having to think about it, like the sense of self. "Obscenity only comes in when the *mind* despises and fears the *body*, and the *body hates* and *resists* the *mind*." These words from an English novel came back to him. Today everything reminded him of this corrosive obscenity. For this reason among many others he wanted to know everything about his divided self, to decipher the true nature of this lack of privacy. Lorna was taking liberties he'd never seen her take before: a kind of animal, exclusive pleasure. With reckless abandon, she granted him only the role of voyeur. Why, incidentally, did he think about those society women dipping their handkerchiefs in Eugen Weidmann's blood at the foot of the guillotine? Something overpowering was blacking out all his reasoning. Never had he felt those tetanic impulses that would have pushed him to commit suicide or murder had they been permanently embedded in him. But his fits of jealousy, self-destructive madness, and patricidal fury barely crossed the line of taboo shared by all normally constituted human beings before he defended himself against them with all his might. Nonetheless, he was determined by whatever means necessary to understand the significance of the slow and uncontrollable anamorphosis—almost a mutation—of his slightest perceptions and desires, as well as his memory that, at certain times of day, took on the mysterious coloring of the ocean floor or an aquarium.

The clock on the Luxembourg Palace chimed six times. Cédric was heading toward the exit closest to the Orangerie. The nurse and the plainclothes agent from the secret service—his "bodyguards," but what body were they guarding?—met near rue de Fleurus while a black sedan parked nearby. No one was waiting for him on rue du Regard. He had been careful not to say anything to the people closest to him, not even to Lorna. His telephone was probably tapped. Under a few items of clothing tossed hastily inside, his suitcase was filled with medicine: antibiotics, sleeping pills, and several small bottles of the immunosuppressive drugs cyclosporine and tacrolimus. A taxi was to pick him up late at night to take him to Charles de Gaulle Airport. He was still a free man with up-to-date identification papers and an autonomous brain. Weren't his rights "natural, inalienable, and sacred"? The enemy was the intrusive matter, all those invasive dreams! Cédric pondered the slice of deep-blue sky above the rooftops. Was there any cure for a disinherited head?

23.

> Airplane crash in Scotland on the night of Wednesday, October 12. A Boeing 727-200 departing from Paris and headed for Reykjavík crashed at about midnight a few hundred yards from Inchgrundle, a town in the north of Scotland, with 149 passengers and 7 crew members aboard. Delayed over an hour at Charles de Gaulle Airport following a minor incident, flight S-413 seems to have left its flight path in order to avoid a severe storm. The causes of the accident remain unclear. No news as yet if there are any survivors.

"Very unlikely!" thought Swen Geislar as he transmitted the night's main dispatch over the agency network before releasing it to the clients: approximately two thousand media outlets throughout France and the Francophone world. He glanced at the zinc rooftops and the boulevard. The light from the streetlamps prolonged a chalky-white dusk. Once again he smiled with obstinate discretion at the thought that nothing until now had come to interfere with his projects: he took on his duties with the restraint of a clergyman, and none of his colleagues dared to laugh at his slight handicap. Rigid in front of his computer screen, he quietly recited a precept of Sun Tzu: "He who excels at war directs the movements of others and does not let anyone dictate his own."

But world news flooded in, and Swen, in the crosshairs of the most violent current events, had the impression that he was a foot soldier holed up under a barrage of universal fire. He steadfastly carried out his drudgery as an intermediary with the fanciful idea of making an insignificant stylistic change, adding or subtracting a word or a slight hyperbole to each of his transmissions. All it took was a comma, an ambiguous synonym, or an uncommon literary allusion. Swen regurgitated the dispatches he received in basic French. His mind haunted by the stunning

Lorna Leer, sometimes he would confess his torment aloud as if he were sleepwalking, all while typing on his keyboard.

> The military skirmish between Turkey and Iran once again risks inflaming the situation in the Middle East. Behind this conflict involving Western geopolitics and interests, some commentators see an unavoidable confrontation between Russia and the United States on the horizon.
>
> One hundred heavy transport vessels carrying tens of thousands of pro-Palestinian militants from all parts of the Western world left the port of Larnaca, in southern Cyprus, on Friday morning in an attempt to break Israel's blockade of the Gaza strip. Jerusalem has promised to "sink this anti-Semitic armada to the bottom of the sea."
>
> An American think tank working for the Pentagon has provided evidence that military action against most terrorist groups would be ineffective. In order to reach this conclusion, researchers analyzed hundreds of thousands of documents regarding 948 terrorist groups identified throughout the world over the past forty years.

> The British Home Office admitted to having "mislaid" the personal data of some 60,000 dangerous prisoners. The encrypted file contained the names of the majority of repeat offenders known for their "prolific criminal behavior" who had to be "monitored as a matter of priority."

Swen's indrawn laughter was more like an asthmatic's coughing fit. He wondered what "prolific criminal behavior" could mean to an Englishman. For a moment, Lorna Leer's face blurred his vision or his screen. He bit his lips and moaned like a wounded puppy. A jumble of sentences filled his mind: "You will keep on forgetting me, whereas I will live in the hell of memory. It's raining but not a drop reaches me. Could it be that I didn't love you enough?"

Swen's confusion lasted only a few seconds. He looked at his watch, then slid his rolling chair away from the metal desk, put on his duffle coat, and crossed the half-empty editorial office in his disjointed robot fashion. In the corridor, above the wide ashen leaves of a rubber tree, a mechanical pendulum clock from another era marked for eternity quarter to twelve. He instinctively checked the time on his watch once again. The weather forecaster, a small bald man with a wide scar that changed colors, called to him in a reedy voice in front of the elevators.

"So? You quitting?"

"Nothing but boring human-interest stories going on," said the stringer. "I'm outta here."

"Let's grab a coffee across the street. I think we have a good fifteen minutes before it starts to pour."

Swen couldn't see how to get out of it. And then, the smell of the coffee at the Vermont was far different from that of the bitter tincture from the office's vending machine. The meteorologist pressed the wrong button, and the upper floors flew by at the speed of a space vessel launcher. By association, Swen recalled the amazing adventure of a German paraglider who was caught in a raging storm and had been sucked up to a height of 32,000 feet. She survived lightning, pounding hailstones, temperatures as low as –60 degrees, and oxygen deprivation. She came down to earth covered in ice and gasping for air, but alive.

At the café counter, the waiter had just knotted his apron around his protruding belly. Sullen, he observed the bluish color of the scar on the man's skull.

"Looks like it's gonna rain!" he remarked in a slightly complicit way, before placing two cups under the coffee machine.

"As you can see," said the meteorologist, "everyone knows my tricks. What was the point of studying the fluid dynamics of the atmosphere for five years? My accident has turned me into a walking barometer."

Swen was fairly new in the office, and he didn't like people confiding in him. He took one of the morning papers set out for customers from the display rack and climbed up on a stool. Nothing on the front page about the airplane crash, which apparently had slipped under the newspapers' radar. He glanced at the obituary page, which began with notice of the death of Morice

Allyn-Weberson: "A giant of the pharmaceutical industry dies," it said, without a single allusion to his family ties to the first man to receive a full body transplant, or to his relation to the beautiful Lorna, whose every move, because he was a genius at doxing and hot reading, and even social engineering, Swen knew by heart.

"I'm going back to my anticyclones," said the weatherman. "Your name is Swen Geislar, isn't it? There was a famous German geographer with that name . . ."

"Must be a great-great uncle . . ."

"My name is Michelet, like the historian. But he wasn't my nephew! You know this one: 'Man is his own Prometheus'"?

As was her habit when she had to go to the news agency offices, Lorna stopped in the Vermont to grab a coffee at the counter and buy a pack of cigarettes and the morning papers. Still on his stool, the stringer counted himself blessed by the gods: only a few feet away, Lorna hadn't noticed his presence. She was dreamily waiting to be served, her eyes flitting across the reflections of a line of bottles and glasses placed against the yellowed mirror at the back of the room. At the risk of being found out, the young man would finally be able to gain standing in her eyes.

"Miss Lorna!" he cried, with the broken smile of a very timid man. "You know, there's important information that even the news agencies miss . . ."

"Oh! It's you, Swen," answered the young woman, whom he'd disturbed in her uneasy torpor.

"Read this," he said, handing her the paper's obituary page. "I think you'll be interested."

Disturbed too abruptly by the implications of the news, Lorna showed no sign of surprise or anger. The forced reserve in which she'd been confined ever since Cédric's inexplicable disappearance, and her anguish, which increased day by day, prevented any reaction in her other than a sudden pallor.

“He was so old,” she murmured distractedly, recalling the billionaire’s emaciated face and the painful notion that he could have offered himself centuries of young beheaded bodies, generation after generation, as fodder for his top-predator immortality.

24.

His face haggard behind dark sunglasses, Cédric rented an Alfa Romeo at the Turin airport in order to arrive as discreetly as possible at San Pedro Hospital. He hadn't forgotten a thing about driving, although it did take him some time to coordinate his gestures, as if two pairs of hands were arguing over how to use the steering wheel. Dr. Aimé Ritz met with him—Cédric was a journalist after all—for yet another interview. Although he had not recognized Cédric, the director of the now famous hospital balked when his visitor began to question him about the donor's identity. The transplant accomplished by Georgio Cadavero and his teams of surgeons at San Pedro had entered the annals of medicine. As for the rest, Ritz, caught off guard, declared that he knew nothing about the body's origin except that it had been delivered by helicopter the day before the operation. Because the administrative services of a hospital that had opened especially for the occasion were at the time not well organized, he hadn't had access to Cédric Allyn-Weberson's file. In any case, doctor-patient confidentiality would have prevented him from divulging anything. "Go question *il signor* Cadavero at Spalline Hospital!" he declared at the end of the interview, as if he were unaware that the neurosurgeon, top sportsman that he was, had just been traded for a small fortune to the Johns Hopkins Hospital in Baltimore.

In Trieste, where Cédric went the next day, Dr. Emil Schoeler was hardly more forthcoming. The hospital he directed had a reputation for discretion and tight security, but because of rivalry with his colleagues in Spalline, Schoeler agreed to meet with the journalist solely on the basis of his press card. When Cédric broached the question of the donor's identity, a circumspect silence seemed the only response possible. Schoeler, who had never ceased denouncing the "celebrification" of the heavyweights of reconstructive surgery, in the end offered a vague path between two points of bioethics. Cédric, paying close attention, allowed the man to hold forth.

"Who worries about human dignity in an era when there is speculation about setting up transplant banks? The concept of brain death does not permit just anything. We know the risks of cerebral angiography. And let's not even talk about body donors! Today, organ-harvesting teams have total leeway to obtain transplant organs very rapidly. Do you really think donors' families are systematically informed in Italy? Most of the time, they're led to believe that treatment is still ongoing, whereas in reality there is no hope."

"Are you implying that the body Georgio Cadavero transplanted could have belonged to someone who didn't want to donate his organs, or that it was used without his family's knowledge?"

"Don't write that!" cried Schoeler. "In my opinion, someone must have procured for Cadavero the body of an accident victim, for example a motorcyclist whose brain had been destroyed; Emergency Rooms get them every day. Still, this body had to correspond perfectly to the criteria posted on the National Hospital Register. This is, of course, only speculation."

Baffled, Cédric dined that evening in a tourist restaurant at the port, then returned straightway to his room in the Kempinski Palace with its immense, illuminated facade overlooking the Gulf of Trieste. With what special privileges and what hope of enlightenment could he begin to visit all the Emergency Rooms in Italy? It was the most ludicrous of whims. He said to himself that Dr. Schoeler, deep within his resentment or his jealousy, had perhaps revealed true information beneath his cautious rhetoric of ambiguous conjecture. In Cedric's position of uncertainty and helplessness, trusting that information was certainly worth the risk.

Lying on the vast, majestic bed, Cédric Erg was overtaken by the specious thoughts and truncated images of drowsiness. He'd felt dizzy and light-headed ever since he'd left Paris. His blood pressure was fluctuating, and several physiological functions were suffering from conflicting impulses, but the ability to move freely somewhat attenuated a sedentary man's hypochondriac obsessions, which, in his situation, were perfectly justified. How could one *not* have somatic symptoms when one was living with someone else's body? Whenever he found himself alone and immobile, his entire being would begin to listen to the enigmatic turmoil of his muscles and organs, from his skin traversed by electric waves to that turbine beating in the cargo hold of night. Then a pounding tremor would pulsate through him, a kind of pain dreamed up in his legitimate body's stead. On the edge of deep sleep, a most horrid tightness would seize him by the throat and, with all his absent strength, he would attempt to return to his former state at the expense of that almost-whole man, there, in this bed, who was demanding cuddles and caresses. Every morning the relentless battle between a ghost and a living corpse would leave him completely shattered. Like a clay figure desperate to be awoken, he would regain his senses, and daylight would catch him by surprise. Something inside him wanted him to move diligently toward an unavoidable revelation.

Having sneaked away like a thief in the night, Cédric hadn't really prepared for a dangerous expedition where every exertion threatened him with myocardial or cerebral infarction. After he'd had breakfast brought to his room so he could swallow a huge quantity of pills in peace, he collected his thoughts in the hotel corridor. No one had recognized him as yet. He'd made sure not to take a cell phone with him. He would be left alone, in the anonymity of crowds, like any other "fetus of a primate having reached sexual maturity." Amused at first by that turn of phrase, Cédric then became worried by the arbitrary way in which his memories were recomposing themselves. He'd lost all familiarity with them as they welled up inside him like counterfeit witnesses to an unknowable past, like previously lived lives.

* * *

On the road to Rome at the wheel of his rental car, he soon felt disoriented. Why was he taking this route rather than another, and what on earth was he going to do in Rome? In the late morning, the heat inside the car became unbearable; unable to figure out how to turn on the air-conditioner, Cédric removed his jacket and shirt with unaccustomed nonchalance. Wearing just a T-shirt, with his solid arms stretched to the steering wheel, he absentmindedly glanced at the scar on his neck in the rearview mirror. The puckered skin fashioned a rosy necklace, and his sweat formed its beads. After hours of driving drowsily, he was hypnotized by the dazzling Tuscan countryside. A balm of light penetrated his skin and his soul. He felt other, different, more lithe, as if he were rejuvenated despite the impression of imminent death that always accompanied him. After he passed Florence, vehicles on the highway went by in clusters, occasionally allowing him time to glance at faces, hundreds of faces passing like a flutter of foam or a cloud. A reflection of his new existence, this phantasmal spectacle shielded him from his former points of reference. Feelings of irreparable exclusion mixed with those of intense inclusion were taking on the shape of the journey. This had become obvious to him as soon as he'd left the rue du Regard. The place where one dwells soon exudes a continuous illusion; above all, that of a body. Now everything was scattered outside of him, leaving only the idea of memories, white traces like a meteor shower. The splendor of the landscape through his windows was slowly buried beneath an absence of images, an incessant dispersal of phosphenes deep in his skull. Similar to cyclonic apparitions on the road, everything continued to disappear in him.

Among these moving, kaleidoscopic fragments, Cédric caught sight of a dubious figure on the roadside. Unsure of himself, he stopped, wanting to make certain that he wasn't dreaming. The hitchhiker ran up to his car and got in next to him without a word, placing his backpack between his legs. As they moved, the muscles of the hitchhiker's bare arms covered in tattoos brought to life an entire population of dragons, centaurs, and other fantastic creatures.

"*Sta guardando il mio tatuaggio?*" asked the man. "*Ne ho anche sulla schiena e sul petto . . .*"

Since the driver indicated that he hadn't understood, the man began to laugh and raised his shirt, pointing to the various interwoven inked chimeras.

"*Un vero museo!*" he went on. "*Lei è inglese? No? Scusa, sarà francese allora! Io, sono siciliano, ma parlo molto bene francese . . .*"

Above the man's left breast, nestled within his chest hairs, Cédric recognized a tattoo similar to the one on his own inner arm. It was an image of three legs with a Medusa head in the middle, surrounded by twigs and stalks of wheat on a purple and ochre background. When he pointed his index finger to the drawing with a questioning look, the man had a curiously defensive response.

"*Il mio paese!*" he shouted. "*La Trinacria, sa? Sulla bandiera della Sicilia.*"

25.

When one is in a foreign country with very little knowledge of its language, one soon finds oneself outside the world. That's what Cédric was saying to himself as he drove off the ferry in his rented car. Scylla and Charybdis had only a mythical resonance: he'd crossed through the Strait without having to choose between a whirlpool and a rock shoal. As he drove beside the high hills where the city of Messina stretches out toward the tip of Calabria, he contemplated the shipyards and military arsenals as they filed by, his mind empty of all representation. He had not really chosen this expedition in Sicily; he had been led there by the intertwining of analogies and coincidences that often accompany a solitary journey. A simple tattoo had sufficed. On the public buildings, next to the Italian flag, one could see waving in the breeze the red and gold gonfalon with its three legs wrapped around each other like an amputated swastika and, in the middle, the flesh-colored Medusa with her crown.

At a traffic circle, Cédric couldn't decide between the road to Trapani-Marsala and the road to Syracuse, the two other tips of the island. The heat caused mists to rise above the sea that had appeared between the docks; bright light shimmered on the asphalt. His face sunburned, his shirt soaking wet, Cédric trusted in the sounds of names and headed southwest. But driving toward Catania and Syracuse, exhausted by hours behind the wheel, he bifurcated instead toward Taormina, on the coast, and inquired about a hotel once he arrived.

An hour later, lying in bed, sheltered by tall shutters through which the sounds of the port filtered, Cédric wondered at length about what he was doing in this room. A stubborn impulse had given him the strength to flee, as if it had been a question of life or death. Nonetheless, he bitterly blamed himself for leaving and for this absurd aimless wandering. From the point of view of sheer common sense, none of this concerned him at all. Without a body of one's own, one no longer dies. He missed simple sensations, Lorna's presence, her sleepy warmth, the morning light on the Paris rooftops, and the silence of things lost. He didn't understand the energy that had been carrying him these past days like a decapitated rooster running away from the chopping block, any more than he did the fundamental disengagement of his mind. In the beauty of the sites he traveled through, the azure bays and the terraced gardens, the cyclopean forests, and the antique ruins on the hills, he saw only a two-dimensional diorama. He despised tourist excursions, except with Lorna, and surely he had gone on them only to please her. His brain burned with a hidden flame in which he could only make out faint glimmers, false memories, or subliminal orders. It's as if I were parasitized, he thought. He'd read articles about the influence of pathogenic germs, arachnids, and other unwelcome guests that survive on a good majority of living species, like the flu virus that modifies human or porcine behavior to its advantage by causing a contagious cough. Or those pond worms that infect other aquatic larvae, which crickets devour once the larvae have left the water; afterward, when the worms have reached adulthood in the crickets' intestines, they take control of the crickets and force them to drown so that the worms can casually carry on their reproductive cycle.

Cédric fluttered his eyelids at the wooden shutters' luminous slits and soon fell to dreaming. Would the atrocious little crustacean that replaces the tongue of the fish it is parasitizing change its accent and its vocabulary? Such a bug that could speak Italian would have been very useful. Or else some polyglot bird fluttering from one mouth to another in order to facilitate universal comprehension. Flocks of sparrows of every color assailed him and tattooed a grimacing Gorgon head on his chest with their beaks.

He awoke with a start in the half-light, a pain in his side, terrified at the thought of dying in this anonymous room. With shaky steps he went to open the blinds on the setting sun. Lights sketched out the silhouette of the hills between the deep-blue sky already studded with stars and the dark shadows rising from the Ionian Sea. Who was he, really? A broken thought could not lay claim to existence, or if it could, it would be solely on the same level as artificial intelligence. He thought back to his college classes on political economy. "It is not consciousness of men that determines their being, but, on the contrary, their social being that determines their consciousness." Reading Karl Marx had destroyed in him any remnant of adolescent Platonism. Today he was nothing but a consciousness without any adherence to things—a state of stupor in search of some intimacy with himself or some sort of harmony. Could it be that he no longer had a soul? Before the transplant, when he was begging to be unplugged, it could only have been in the deranged desire for a world beyond. One commits suicide only for a better life. But hope no longer had any physical substance, no body! What mother or lover would ever come to tell him a tale of never-ending love and enchantment? From this point on, he would perceive death as a kind of insomnia, dreary and deaf, where one is divested of the use of one's senses, infinitely more frightening than the eve of an execution. And in fact he waited for dawn without turning his gaze from the lights offshore.

Early the next morning, Cédric got back on the road to Syracuse, hurrying in a way that was unusual for him. His intention of visiting all the hospitals in Sicily now seemed only slightly less eccentric than his presence on the island. Before him, slipping from right to left according to the twists in the road, Mount Etna soon held all his attention: immense, similar to Mount Fuji, which he had seen in the past, with at the highest crater a bluish smoke in the shape of double horns. He thought back to other things he'd read: to the madman from Agrigento, to those slow-moving monsters with their countless hands, faces without necks, arms wandering without shoulders, unattached, and eyes straying alone, in need of foreheads; to the offspring of oxen with the heads of men and men with the heads of oxen. Empedocles' correct prophecies before he tumbled into the eternal bath of lava! Would it not be possible from now on to "course along through one another," to become those mixed creatures "furnished with sterile parts"?

When he reached the volcano, Cédric forgot all about Syracuse and left the highway, turning toward the coast in the direction of Catania. It was the second-largest city on the island. Why not try his luck there rather than somewhere else? Though he seemed to have lost his mind, he had regained his mobility. The sun's strong rays no longer bothered him. He'd been warned about the risks of melanoma and carcinoma as a result of his immunosuppressant treatment, so he protected his face above all. After parking the Alfa Romeo beneath the shade of a plane tree, decked out in a panama hat he'd bought along the way and dark sunglasses, he wandered for quite some time along the deserted streets of the center city. At the emergency services of Cannizzaro Hospital, he ludicrously blurted out some words in his paltry Italian to the male nurses who were smoking between the ambulance ramps and the swinging doors that led to the operating room. One of them, who knew a few words of French, thought he was dealing with an escapee from the psychiatric ward.

"*Signore,* we see many, many road accident victims every day! *Andate pure a richiedere all'amministrazione.*"

In Vittorio Emanuele II Hospital, he was greeted with the same awkward suspicion. Cédric returned to his car and got lost in the arid hills dominated by Mount Etna. He drove aimlessly between the volcano and the sea, oppressed by the heat. He returned through other twisted streets in the lower city; a maze of dark alleyways around churches, theaters, and monumental fountains replaced the tiered baroque palaces. Again he drove along the piers of the port basins; the volcanic rock of the shoreline bore witness to devastating eruptions. After the black sand beaches and Ognina Gulf, he saw the muddy waters amid the marshes stretching out in front of him. An inn overlooking the water caught his eye. So he would take refuge in the Oasis at the mouth of the Simeto River. After parking the Alfa Romeo beneath the arbors, Cédric took his luggage, convinced he had reached the end of his somnambulistic circumambulation.

In the inn's hallway, a reproduction of Piero della Francesca's Saint Agatha carrying her severed breasts on a platter hung between the counter and the staircase. A female dwarf with enormous thighs wearing a man's cap burst from a broom closet and found the visitor in contemplation in front of the painting.

"*A Catania,*" she said, "*amiamo i seni di sant'Agata anche come dolci.*"

26.

"To keep within thy dumb heart," muttered Cédric under his breath as he was expelled from a dream of absolute exile on a desert island. "To keep within thy dumb heart," he repeated, sitting up and leaning on his elbows. What on earth could it mean?

After three days of lethargy behind closed shutters, naked beneath the huge ceiling fan that roared like an airplane, he admitted to himself that his reclusion had gone on long enough. Sleeping day and night between meals eaten in his room in an inn full of summer vacationers would soon make him appear suspect. And then, he was becoming stiff; the aches of an old man were plaguing his neck. The sound of the telephone woke him completely. The female dwarf with the cap said he had a call from *Parigi*. A voice garbled by static replaced hers a few seconds later.

"Cédric, can you hear me?"

He remained silent, torn between a rather affectless kernel of joy and a mixed feeling of artifice and disloyalty.

"Your father died last Monday. He was buried yesterday in Geneva. Can you hear me? You have to come back. Everyone's looking for you."

"My father? Dead? Is that really you, Lorna?" he exclaimed, as if he were recollecting a world that had vanished eons ago.

"You've got to get on a plane and come back as soon as possible. You're in danger in Catania."

"How did you find out where I was?"

"Turin, Trieste, Rome, Sicily? Through your credit card; it's not complicated. And then, a missing person alert was sent out. Your picture has been in all the media since yesterday. Georgio Cadavero said on American TV that he feared you'd been abducted. He's not mistaken. You probably have a price on your head. Now there are two teams of assassins on your heels, and they may be the same ones who . . ."

"Where are you? I don't understand what you're saying."

"I'll explain everything when I see you. Hide as best you can. I'll come to get you wherever you are. You are in grave danger, understand?"

Lorna had time to reveal what his father had told her in Versoix. The accident on the *Evasion* was no doubt an attempted homicide. Cédric had been a target not only because he was the heir to the M.A.W. laboratories but also because he was a polemicist, the archenemy of the pharmaceutical industry and the oil corporations. Their communication was interrupted by a piercing whistling sound after she'd said, "But there's something else . . ."

Facing the bathroom mirror, still naked, he stared at his indurated scar, as thick as a hangman's rope. His features had changed since the transplant. A facial plastic surgeon had spoken to him about autoplastic transformations linked to trauma, age, or madness. Cédric would end up losing any and all resemblance to himself, both physical and moral. What was happening in him could almost be a blank psychosis, a kind of factual schizophrenia. He'd become an object of study, one of those severed heads that Géricault procured from the Paris morgue in order to paint them in his studio. This virile body below him was no more than a clever prosthesis or an illusory décor. At least it would allow him to get away: he'd had enough of Catania. He would head to Syracuse as soon as possible.

In the hallway, suitcase in hand, Cédric left a generous tip for the staff, who, oddly, rushed to say good-bye to him. Emerging from her broom closet, the dwarf grabbed his forearm so forcefully that her cap fell to the floor.

"*È lei, il trapiantato!*" she cried. "*Che onore per la nostra istituzione. Permettici di prendere una foto di voi davanti all'hotel . . .*"

Cédric fled from the chaos, terrified. With the Oasis of the Simeto River behind him, he avoided going back into the city and instead took a side road that led to the highway. What had Lorna meant on the phone? What other danger must he fear besides imploding because of an asymptomatic acute rejection? A hybrid subject, a nebulous artifact of himself, he knew everything about the dirty tricks that medical science had in store for him.

Speeding through the deserted streets at the wheel of his Alfa Romeo, Cédric rapidly arrived near the volcano. The sun was at its zenith. The mountain in front of him quivered in the blazing air. At the first crossroad, a roadblock set up by the mobile brigade of the Catania Police Force obliged him to stop. The officers apologized when they discovered he was an ordinary French tourist. One of them mentioned the "bad families" in the region, the trafficking, the assassinations. They didn't even ask to see his papers. Nonetheless the incident upset him and he made a wrong turn; now he was driving down a one-way street toward the city center. He became feverish, as if he were scalded; the sweat from the nape of his neck and his body collected around his scar. In Catania, he disappeared down the alleyways of the port where the bright light contrasted with the slices of night between the facades. When he got to via Etnae, a burning thirst forced him to park the car at the corner of a large pedestrian square where scattered groups were strolling. Without thinking, he staggered over to the dripping marble basin crowned with an elephant carrying an obelisk of volcanic rock, and he dived in halfway, torso first. He felt faint, and then lost consciousness amid the spurting fountains. The crowd, intrigued, began to form a circle around him, and it wasn't until a child shouted that a man was drowning that someone came to his rescue. A person who claimed to be qualified to give first aid unbuttoned Cédric's shirt, and he was naked to the waist in front of everyone, with, around his neck and throat, that awful, rubbery, wine-colored scar. When he came to, the faces leaning over him showed more curiosity than repulsion, along with a sort of mistrust of the drunkard or madman who had just made an exhibition of himself. Some people were looking at him out of the corner of their eye with an impudent, presumptuous expression. Had they recognized him as the creature of those modern Frankensteins? A young brunette wearing a fitted black dress fished his sunglasses out of the basin and placed them in his hands with a reverential air, as if the glasses were his living eyes. Cédric, on his feet again, buttoned up his shirt. Awkwardly taking leave of the impromptu audience that had formed under the spreading shade of the elephant, he fled toward via Etnae as an ambulance siren wailed nearby. His hair still dripping, he was about to reach his car, more tormented by all those gazes than by his bout of heatstroke, when the young brunette from the fountain approached him.

"I recognized you," she murmured in halting French. "You're the man from Turin. The one who . . ."

She was unable to finish her sentence. Her eyes, the color of gold or sulfur, grew wide, and she made a small, ambiguous gesture with her right hand, as if to signify throat slitting or decapitation. Tears streamed down her face. Was she the saint of Catania, a fugitive from the cathedral's reliquary, the virgin with her breasts torn off come to console the poor sinner with his corpseless head? Both frightened and amused, Cédric dimly recalled a poem by Apollinaire. He asked the woman what she wanted, perturbed by her physical closeness, a few inches from his face in the scorching sun. What was that famous poem?

"I know who you are," she said, using the informal *tu* before she quickly retreated to the formal *vous*. "In fact, in a way I was expecting you. It had to happen, it just had to . . ."

Cédric looked at her without hearing her, both moved by her vixen-like beauty and deeply saddened by the tragic, quivering light, the scent of incense and dried roses the churches exuded, and this world without reference points. Then two lines of poetry came back to him:

> Farewell Farewell
> Sun corpseless head.

27.

Cédric was barely conscious of what had happened to him directly after his fainting spell, as if he'd been drunk or under the influence of psychotropic drugs. He could remember it only in a diffuse way, in snatches, but these snatches had the intensity of certain dreams more radiant than any waking state. Anantha had led him through a maze of backstreets and stairways. "It's as cool as the inside of a church at my place. You'll be able to rest," she whispered in his ear, as she took him by the arm. He was convinced it was absolutely vital to take his luggage with him. At last they arrived in Librino, a working-class neighborhood of Catania. Was his clouded reasoning a result of his inability to control his breathing? In order for him to regulate it, the air he breathed would have had to be his own. But nothing belonged to him by rights, no use or enjoyment of this body. His brain was dealing with another endocrine system; what can one hundred billion neurons do faced with a flood of hormones? The molecular mechanisms of pharmaceutics tended to stabilize his organ regulation systems at the expense of his mind.

He'd finally understood that the immunosuppressant treatments were targeting his head; his head was the graft, the non-self! He even had to readapt sounds for himself, turn them into magic words, like the long-drawn-out echo of some other understanding.

How many days or weeks had he been living cloistered in Anantha's bedroom? The notion of time demands some control over one's sensations. But time and space escaped him. Half unconscious, a thing watching itself become a thing among the thousand arms of a shadow, he was experiencing a kind of ecstasy or slow torture. For Anantha had seized him without scruples, madly, like a she-wolf grabs a small man. She was a tall, loose-limbed woman with firm breasts below a dark face; her eyes looked like they had been lined with ink, staring, immense. Even before glimpsing the Gorgon tattooed on his arm, she'd recognized him lying unconscious beneath the volcanic rock elephant. Blood pulsated between them at first sight. She had seized this desirable body like a carnivore, biting its skin all the way to the scar, licking, delving into the grooves of its muscles with her lips and tongue, swallowing the fingers and the penis, rubbing the offering of her moist sex against its thighs and hands. What to do in the lonely night with blind eyes? "Alessandro!" she would cry, then become silent, shuddering. She repeated this name again and again behind the haunted half-light of the shutters, in the muffled rumble of the night. Then, sitting up abruptly, her hair a-tumble, she would sob, clinging to the body, scratching the chest, her inky eyes riven to the narrow site of unstable flesh. "*Mai più ci separeremo,*" she would say a hundred times, shaking her head. "*Mai più, amore mio!*"

Stunned by the hallucinatory vision of her

lover's bare body at the base of the fountain, Anantha found refuge in the stubborn silence of sensuality. She didn't recognize the voice as Alessandro's, but the solid arms were indeed his; she felt his penis unfurl in her fingers, and smelled the soothing scent of his armpits. She went over every inch of his skin, the least little beauty mark, the folds and tiny wrinkles. She rubbed her full breasts against his buttocks, pressing her lips and her entire face wet with saliva in the small of his back and along the double muscular furrow on either side of the spine. She whispered unknown words against his heart, right between the ribs, and into his large open hands, to the veins beating in his wrist and groin. She begged this stiff shaft to drive into her, to penetrate her as deeply as possible, to make her a child.

Hour after hour, neck on the pillow, the abandoned head experienced a mixture of painful impulses, flashes of images, snatches of dreams or thoughts all held captive in a muck of bodily sensations. As soon as dawn broke, a continuous beating would shake the ground, like the turbines and boilers of a cargo ship on a sea to nowhere. The nights sped by and seemed to rustle with the panting of countless bats hanging from the joists. Apparently there were no neighbors. The apartment must have been located above a workshop of some sort—perhaps a blacksmith's, or a foundry. A service staircase probably led to a finished attic. Keys in hand, naked under her fitted dress that she could quickly slip out of, Anantha came and went. She brought back food, alcohol, and cigarettes. He had never known a hungrier lover. But in her impatience to touch her hostage's flesh with her own, a look of panic or terror disfigured her. Anantha was always slightly drunk on a dark-red wine she poured from straw-covered bottles. Whenever she would drink glass after glass in front of him, there would come a moment when she'd begin to sob, repeating over and over: "I know you don't drink, Alessandro, *che non hai mai bevuto una goccia di alcol, mai, mai . . .*"

One morning when his mind was a little clearer, Cédric realized that he must be being drugged, or else a lethal process was alienating him from this body's neurovegetative system, from this body's idiosyncrasy, which was gradually reinstating itself in its massive primacy. What remained of Cédric's free will? Could he still think on his own, through all the instinctive movements and inner sensations from which he was receiving bizarre, foreign signals? He had once read obscure articles on the abdomen's intellect, the famous Japanese *hara,* a sort of spirit of the flesh in contrast to the cerebral firmament. Ever since he'd been under the influence of this land, dazzled prisoner of a widow or a volcano, he'd felt as if he were reflected at his own expense, the object of some unformulated intention. Can one escape from such a struggle? In a merciless battle, a part of him was being abandoned to this slow, living enterprise, to the invading hysteria of muscles and organs. How could he doubt that Alessandro's beheaded body, as an unthinking plunderer, would make use of words and images that belonged by rights to his memory?

When his jailer Anantha left him on his own, sometimes he would pull himself out of his lethargy and totter around in the dim light of the venetian blinds. For him, the rooms had a paradoxical intimacy related to their foreignness. In one room, crowded with furniture and trunks, he found a photo album. Anantha was smiling in the pictures, cheerful, without that fever in her eyes. In other pictures, he had no trouble identifying Alessandro in biker's clothes, a helmet under his arm, or in a bathing suit on an Italian beach. It was indeed the same body with its broad chest and narrow waist, and the arm tattooed with the bluish triskelion. Cédric's fascination ended up changing into a fleeting sense of déjà vu. Yet the man hardly resembled him. His features were rather feminine; blue eyes and long hair, furrowed brow and slightly tensed lips. Among the numerous elements that had to correspond, such as height, girth, blood type, and allergies, the appearance of the face was quite obviously not a requirement for a compatible body. Obsessing over this face that he, in some horrible way, was replacing within strict constraints, Cédric couldn't help falling under the spell of so much virile candor, nor could he repress an indefinable sense of annoyance—anger almost—at the sight of that face. Whenever Anantha would grab onto the living body of her beloved, she would avoid all contact with the foreign head, most often covering it with part of a sheet. Although he felt as if he were on the sidelines of this mysterious lovemaking, Cédric nonetheless experienced something of its pleasure in the recesses of his brain.

A front view of Alessandro with bare shoulders engrossed him until he lost all notion of his own presence, sinking into Alessandro with the rapt repulsion that the suicidal feel for the void or deep water. This savage back-and-forth between a head and a body made him dizzy. From now on, he was inevitably fated to be deprived of existence. Was he even alive? His skull rolled endlessly at the foot of a chopping block of flesh and bones. On an organic level, he was indeed this other who was flooding him with too-thick blood and other bodily fluids, imposing on him his cardiac rhythm and his fevers. Cédric, frantic and befuddled, wondered how to escape from such a nightmare, as horrifying when he touched his scar as it was sickly sweet in the swarthy arms of this love-struck widow with her ink-lined eyes.

Another time Cédric found a pile of old newspaper clippings in a shoebox. Anantha had kept all the articles from the *Quotidiano di Sicilia* that dealt with Alessandro Branci's accident. He could be seen both smiling in his biker's clothes and in the Emergency Room of a hospital in Catania. Cédric read every clipping attentively. The accident had occurred on a coastal road between the sea and the volcano on July 7 of the previous year—in other words, the day before the transplant in Turin; Alessandro had been taken in an ambulance to Principessa Jolanda Hospital, where the surgeons had declared him brain dead. An ordinary accident. The biker was driving in a drunken state. His blood-alcohol level was extremely high. From another box Cédric took out I.D. papers, an expired passport with Alessandro's height, eye color, and place of birth, and two visas for neighboring Tunisia. The passport photo, sharper than the one in the newspaper, affected Cédric physically with a terrible itching around his scar.

"*Non è grazioso, signore!*" shouted Anantha, who, coming back home, caught him in the middle of his investigations.

As she shut the door, panic-stricken, she refrained from telling him that a woman—a journalist who'd come from France—was desperately searching for him in town; nor did Anantha mention the fact that she'd chased that woman away from the factory doorstep as if she were a criminal.

Cédric turned with open arms toward Anantha, his hands full of press clippings. He suddenly intuited that his fate depended on the goodwill of this wild-eyed vixen and the people around her. How had he ever managed to reach her, by what involuntary motive, what obscure meanderings of desire? He no longer even knew where he'd come from; a fever was drowning his last memories. Paris, Geneva, or Rome—the great stage sets of his memory were crumbling, vanishing around him. He would never be able to leave this island. Lorna was no longer anything but a longing inside him, without substance, barely real. The machine tools of the factory suddenly stopped shaking the ground. From the depths of the body or the night, an unfamiliar song was rising. "To keep within thy dumb heart," he thought he heard when the evening silence breathed heavily in his ears.

"They're coming to kill you," the young woman whispered quickly, as she poured herself a glass of Chianti. "They've been paid to do it, the ones from the family, *padre e figli*. You have to leave now, immediately! Go as far as you possibly can!"

Anantha, nervous, her eyes dark, poured herself more wine even before her glass was empty and began to laugh bitterly. Because a dead man could be desired to the point of madness, why couldn't he be killed? She began to tremble, and her eyes now shone with tears.

"Alessandro didn't drink!" she cried. "*Alessandro, non hai mai bevuto una goccia di alcol, mai, mai . . .*"

Epilogue

Ever at his post as foot soldier, Swen Geislar was retranscribing, in his precise, covert way, today's news as it flooded in from the entire world. None of the news agency's correspondents who were in contact with him paid any attention to him, putting his little whims down to his concern for concision. Distracted by a flight of crows, Swen glanced at the zinc rooftops of the boulevard des Italiens. A steady rain made them shine like a mirror beneath the leaden light. And dispatches also rained down on his desktop.

> An Austrian team has perfected a bionic hand controlled by the brain that provides advantages similar to those of a transplant and is able to do a variety of everyday tasks. According to Dr. Aszmann, bionic reconstruction is less risky than the hand transplant that has been performed since

1997, which requires taking very strong immunosuppressant medication and often resulted in the need to re-amputate the patient.

A new leak of radioactive water, with radiation levels of up to one hundred times greater than those that have been recorded since the catastrophe, was detected this morning on the site of the Japanese nuclear reactor in Fukushima, according to TEPCO.

An international team, including scientists from the Astrophysics Department-AIM and the Particle Physics Department of CEA-Irfu, has just used the Mega-Planck satellite to discover galaxy clusters upon clusters upon clusters with characteristics that were previously unknown. Located extremely far away from us, the clusters of clusters of clusters that group up to a thousand galaxy clusters of clusters are the largest structures in the universe. Astrophysicists were able to detect the new clusters thanks to the imprint left in the background radiation of the universe by the hot gas from the clusters. Of the 389 clusters detected by Mega-Planck at distances from 5 to 10 billion light-years, most were previously unknown.

Swen sighed in dismay at the exhausting diversity of the information he received—countless articles in that vast encyclopedia of current affairs that the media machinery churned out night and day. What was the role of the intermediary drudge in all this? By changing a word from time to time, there was of course the possibility of keeping oneself amused.

The discovery of human meat in the Pindu brand of lasagna, which was supposed to contain beef, caused a scandal in the UK—where man is revered and eating him is taboo—and led to the withdrawal Friday in France and Belgium of the suspected products. Human meat was found in large quantities in the UK (up to 100%) in the Pindu lasagna of a Romanian producer, the president of the Cadigel company—which owns the Pindu brand—explained to investigators. It was determined that it came from slaughterhouses in the Timisoara region, which slaughtered and cut up both beef and humans, he added.

But for David Cameron, this story is "shocking and entirely unacceptable." It creates a problem of "confidence," he said from Brussels. In the UK, the

> affair also takes on a cultural dimension: human meat is normally unavailable in stores, unlike in France and Switzerland, where it is esteemed for its tenderness. In the UK, the country par excellence for the sport of foot racing, man is one of the main recipients of the animals' Victoria Cross, the highest award of the United Kingdom honors system.

Just for a laugh, Swen was about to send the reworked dispatch to his meteorologist colleague Michelet, when news retransmitted from Palermo popped up on his screen and went straight to his heart. He didn't give a damn about the "tragic end of the first man to receive a total body transplant," but Lorna, Lorna! How could he survive a single day without the only woman he'd ever even dreamed of loving? Nonetheless, he pulled himself together, his eyes already dry. The great reporter from the news agency who had been parachuted into every corner of this apocalyptic world was not a woman to let herself get caught, not even by the Cosa Nostra! A slim hope caused him to scroll through the news with a trembling finger.

The murder of the man who received the first full body transplant and his companion has caused considerable consternation in the medical research and financial worlds. Cédric Allyn-Weberson was found atrociously mutilated inside a rented Alfa Romeo on a Sicilian coastal road. The sole heir of a recently deceased wealthy Swiss businessman, he disappeared from his Paris home on June 30. While there is no question that La Stidda was involved, the motives for this double homicide remain unclear. Was Cédric Allyn-Weberson a hostage of the local mafia? Could he have survived without his specialized medication? Did his jailors assassinate him, as often happens when a ransom is not paid? Another trail concerns Lorna Leer, the man's companion. It will be recalled that Leer, an investigative journalist, had openly implicated a consortium of pharmaceutical laboratories regarding an attempted homicide of Cédric Allyn-Weberson. Having landed the day before the tragedy at the international airport in Catania, she had just recorded and broadcast on a news site the testimony of an anesthesiologist nurse from Principessa Jolanda Hospital whose name we will not reveal. This nurse stated that a victim of a motorcycle accident transported to the

> Emergency Room two days before the fabled transplant in Turin showed no visible lesions on arrival, but seemed rather to be under the influence of a hypnotic sedative such as propofol or etomidate before he was declared to be brain dead following a disastrous surgical procedure. The possible relationship between these comments and the execution by beheading of the well-known transplant recipient is still unknown. Only his head was found at the feet of Lorna Leer, who had been killed by a bullet to the head at the wheel of the Alfa Romeo. The steep ransom that most likely was impossible to pay under the circumstances leads one to suspect collusion between the hostage takers and the assassins, with their highly placed backers in the business world. Europol and the Italian criminal police are investigating, together with the Carabinieri, in order to get to the bottom of a mystery that grows deeper by the hour.

“Unbelievable!” cried Swen. That blabbermouthed nurse, that whole story about the mafia and the manhunt, and the kidnappers who were paid more to murder their hostage than to free him! Wasn't one of his small roles at the news agency in fact to establish the pertinence and authenticity of each and every dispatch before writing it up? And this one, he believed, was sorely lacking the slightest credibility.

Hubert Haddad is a Franco-Tunisian novelist, poet, playwright, short story writer, and essayist. He has received literary prizes for a number of his publications, including the 2008 Prix des Cinq Continents de la Francophonie and the 2009 Prix Renaudot Poche for *Palestine,* a compelling political novel. Published in seven languages, *Palestine* is currently being adapted into a motion picture. His latest novel to be translated into English, *Rochester Knockings,* was published in 2015.

Alyson Waters is a translator of modern and contemporary French and Francophone literary fiction. She has translated works by Vassilis Alexakis, Louis Aragon, Emmanuel Bove, Albert Cossery, Jean Giono, Daniel Pennac, and Tzvetan Todorov, among others. Waters has received several grants and prizes for her translations, including, in 2012, the French-American Foundation and Florence Gould Foundation Translation Prize for Eric Chevillard's *Prehistoric Times.*